Albert's
Old House

Daphne Neville

Copyright © 2022 Daphne Neville

All rights reserved, including the right to reproduce this book, or portions thereof in any form. No part of this text may be reproduced, transmitted, downloaded, decompiled, reverse engineered, or stored, in any form or introduced into any information storage and retrieval system, in any form or by any means, whether electronic or mechanical without the express written permission of the author.

This is a work of fiction. Names and characters are the product of the author's imagination and any resemblance to actual persons, living or dead, is entirely coincidental.

The views expressed in this work are solely those of the author and do not necessarily reflect the views of the publisher, and the publisher hereby disclaims any responsibility for them.

ISBN: 9798360861713

PublishNation
www.publishnation.co.uk

Other Titles by This Author

TRENGILLION CORNISH MYSTERY SERIES
The Ringing Bells Inn
Polquillick
Sea, Sun, Cads and Scallywags
Grave Allegations
The Old Vicarage
A Celestial Affair
Trengillion's Jubilee Jamboree

PENTRILLICK CORNISH MYSTERY SERIES
The Chocolate Box Holiday
A Pasty in a Pear Tree
The Suitcase in the Attic
Tea and Broken Biscuits
The Old Bakehouse
Death by Hanging Basket
Murder in Hawthorn Road
Great Aunt Esme's Pasty Shop

The Old Coaching Inn
The Old Tile House

Chapter One

"Nearly there," Dilys Granger, known to everyone as Dilly, waved her hand towards a row of houses. "I remember those houses, you see because I stopped there to ask for directions and a very nice young man drew me a little map. He then asked if I was interested in buying Lavender Cottage and when I told him I was his eyebrows shot up." She chuckled, "I suppose he thought I was far too old to do up a dilapidated old house."

"Dilapidated! You told me it just needs a bit of TLC." Freddie briefly took his eyes off the road and glanced at his seventy-two year old godmother sitting by his side.

"And so it does. It just needs a bit of updating and modernisation, especially to the kitchen. I'll need to install central heating too and a bit of plumbing work will need doing. Apart from that it's in tip-top condition and is structurally sound. Lovely thick walls too so nice and cosy."

After turning into and along several more streets and finally onto a road running along the sea front, Dilly asked Freddie to slow down. "There, that's it," she squealed, both arms flapping, "Over there. The one with the green door."

Freddie took his foot off the accelerator and pulled up alongside the pavement in front of two semi-detached houses. Both were granite built and between them an enclosed entry led to the rear of the properties.

"Oh, isn't it beautiful." Dilly jumped down from the passenger seat of the hired van onto the pavement and rested her hands on emerald green railings that ran along the front of both gardens; grinning like a Cheshire cat she gazed lovingly at her new home. "I can't believe how much the dahlias have grown. Their shoots were only just peeping through the earth when I first viewed the house. Now they're in full flower and looking delightful."

Freddie gazed around in awe. "The location certainly is beautiful. I know you said you had sea views but never guessed you were this close." As he closed the door of the van, a woman emerged from the adjoining house. "My dear, you're back. So lovely to see you again," she kissed Dilly on both cheeks and then looked at Freddie, "and who's this lovely young man?"

"This is Freddie, my godson who has very kindly driven me down here with all my worldly goods."

"Delighted to meet you, Freddie. I am Amelia Trewella, your godmother's new next door neighbour and I live here at Yew Tree Cottage." She waved her hand towards her home.

"Good to meet you too." Freddie stepped back to avoid a kiss.

Amelia glanced at the van. "I take it you've left your car behind."

Dilly chuckled. "Yes, but then I had no choice. It failed its MOT dismally last week and would have cost an arm and a leg to fix so it went for scrap. I might get myself a little run-around eventually but on the other hand I might not. After all the bus service here is pretty good and I don't expect I'll be gadding out much anyway."

"Yes, we don't go out much as there's no need. We have our groceries delivered weekly and everything else is available on-line. I do like to potter round the charity shops when I go into town though."

"Sounds like fun." Dilly stepped down from the pavement onto the path that separated the two front gardens. "Everything is looking lovely. Have you been tending my garden as well as your own? Because I can't believe it would look that good without a helping hand."

"Yes, I've done a bit of weeding, dead-heading and staking. I hope you don't mind, it's just that dear old Bert did so love his dahlias and I couldn't bear to see them neglected."

"Of course I don't mind. In fact I'm very grateful. It's a shame the lavender has gone over though but I should imagine it looked superb back in the summer."

"It did. Dear Bert, lavenders weren't his favourite flowers but his mother loved them and so he continued to grow them in her memory."

"Was it his mother who named the house then?" Freddie asked.

"No, it was actually his grandmother, Elizabeth Bray, but Bert's mother had always admired them and so was happy to continue growing them after her mother-in-law passed away."

"That's really nice and I shall continue the tradition," said Dilly.

"Well, I hope you have better luck than me. I've tried to grow them but they always failed and I can't believe the soil in Bert's garden, your garden, is any different to mine and the climate certainly isn't. Lavender likes it hot and dry which I'm afraid is something not to be relied on in Cornwall."

"Hmm, interesting so perhaps a touch of divine intervention helped Bert, his mother and grandmother along."

"A lovely idea," chuckled Amelia, "albeit completely bonkers."

Albert Bray, known to everyone as Bert, was the erstwhile owner occupant of Lavender Cottage. He had lived in the house since he was ten years old when his parents had inherited the property on the death of his widowed grandfather, George Bray. A builder by trade,

Albert had long since retired. His love was his garden and in particular his dahlias which he had tended with love for many years adding to and replacing varieties when necessary. At the age of eighty-seven he looked as fit as he had done thirty years before. It came as a shock therefore when he was taken ill and died within twenty-four hours of hospital admission. His will was stored at the office of his solicitor and with no living close family all were surprised to discover he requested the house be sold on his demise and after all bills were settled the remaining monies be donated to the village church. The reason for the surprise was because apart from the occasional funeral, Bert had not set foot in the church since his childhood when attendance at the village school's carol service was compulsory.

"Would you like me to give you a hand unloading your stuff?" Amelia asked, "I'd be more than willing and I'm pretty strong."

"Thank you, yes, but first we need to make room for it."

"Make room for it?" Freddie blurted. "Surely there's more than enough room in there for your modest amount of furniture."

"Oh, yes there is but not until we've shifted things around a bit." Dilly noticed her godson's frown. "Bert's stuff is still in the house, Freddie. Didn't I tell you that?" Freddie shook his head. "Oh silly me. It's still there you see because I bought the place lock, stock and barrel. Thought it'd save the church or whoever sorting it out and I hated the thought of the poor old boy's stuff being taken to the tip."

"And don't worry, young man," Amelia reassured him. "Bert didn't have a great deal of furniture anyway. He seldom used his front room and lived very frugally."

"Come on," Dilly urged Freddie, "I'll show you around and then you'll be able to see what's what."

"Would you mind awfully if I came too? I'd love to have a peep inside because in the ten years Ernie and I have lived next door I've only ever been in the living room and even then only on a couple of occasions. Bert kept himself very much to himself and most of our little chit-chats took place in either the back or front gardens."

"Of course I don't mind, Amelia. It'd be interesting to hear any comments you might have."

Dilly took the key she had picked up at the estate agents from her pocket and unlocked the green front door. As she stepped into a square hallway, Freddie and Amelia followed.

Two doors, one to the left painted lime green and the other to the right painted chocolate brown, led from either side of the hall. Opposite coats hung from a row of pegs and a steep, straight staircase ran to the upper floor.

"Isn't this lovely?" gushed Dilly, pointing to a rag rug part covering the red tiled floor, "I bet it was made by Bert's mother. Rug making was very popular in the fifties due to austerity brought about by the war years and using cut up rags was a cheap way of doing it."

"Oh yes," agreed Amelia, "I recall us having several during my childhood, lovingly made by my dear old mum."

Freddie closed the front door. "Dark in here," he grumbled, "now the door's shut the only bit of light is coming from upstairs."

"I was just thinking that," agreed Amelia, "Anyway, which room shall we go in first?"

"This one," Dilly opened the brown door which had a step down into a spacious room, sparsely furnished with a single misshapen beam running the entire length of the plastered ceiling.

"Very nice," said Freddie, "and two windows facing the sea. Lovely."

"This is what Bert called the front room," said Amelia, "I've not been in here before but I've peeped through the windows occasionally when he was out."

"I love the doors here," Dilly ran her hand over the paintwork, "they so cottagey and they all have latches too which make lovely clunking noises. In fact it was partly them that sold the house to me. They remind me of my childhood, you see."

"They're plank doors," said Freddie, airing his building knowledge, "and I agree, they're very much in keeping with the place."

When they were ready they went back into the hallway and into the room with the line green door.

"The living room," said Amelia, "and this fascinates me. It's like stepping into a time capsule. Look at that kitchen cabinet. I remember my parents having one back in the fifties and sixties. In fact everybody did back then before fitted kitchens became the rage."

"And a Rayburn too," said Freddie, approvingly, "that should make it cosy in here during the winter months."

"Actually, it's a Truburn," said Dilly, "but no doubt the same principle." She stepped towards it. "And look, behind these boarding sheets must be the original fireplace. I'm longing to see it and expose it in the fullness of time."

On either side of the boarded up chimney breast were seated recesses. On one sat an ancient radio; the other was stacked with books.

"Was Bert musical?" Freddie lifted the lid of a piano and pressed a few keys; they were hopelessly out of tune.

"Ouch! Not if he played that," laughed Dilly.

"I commented on that when I first saw it," said Amelia, "but it was his mother who played. He couldn't play himself and felt he ought to find a new home for it but was reluctant to do so as it was his mother's pride and joy."

"In that case it must stay," said Dilly, "I shall get it tuned and take good care of it."

"Can you play then?" Amelia asked.

"A bit but I'm not very good. Having said that when this place is shipshape I'll have plenty of time to brush up my meagre skills."

As Freddie closed the piano lid, Dilly picked up a framed photograph of a brass band. "Any family members on this, Amelia?"

"Oh yes, that's Bert," she pointed to a young man on the front row holding a trumpet, "I don't think the band exists now but Bert was a loyal member for a good many years and always spoke of it with great affection and said how he missed it. Apparently he left after his parents died."

"I see," Dilly returned the picture to the sideboard and then pointed to a framed sepia photograph of a rotund lady hanging above the television set. It looked to have been taken in a studio setting; a heavy curtain hung in the background and on a table beside the lone figure stood a vase of lavender, "And who might this lady be?"

"Probably Ethel, Bert's mum, although maybe not as it looks before her time." Amelia took the picture from the wall, turned it over and read the inscription. "Ah, it's Elizabeth Bray. Bert's grandmother."

"And the lady who named this house," said Dilly, "hence the lavenders. She really must have had a passion for them."

Freddie looked over Amelia's shoulder. "She looks a bit austere."

"On no, I think she has a kindly face," said Dilly, "and I'm sure, were she still around, she and I would have a lot in common."

As Amelia returned the picture to the wall, Freddie leaned on the window sill and looked outside. "This room is also on the front of the house with views of the sea, the same as the front room, so why did Bert call the other room the front room?"

Amelia shrugged her shoulders. "I daresay it's what his parents would have called it. Things were simpler back-along. People didn't call sitting rooms lounges and only the toffs had drawing rooms, studies, parlours and what have you. Anyway, it's not just a living room because Bert used it as a kitchen too as did his mother before him."

"But if this was used as a kitchen where's the sink?" Freddie opened a door beside a solid electric cooker and found he was looking into an under stairs cupboard with a small window facing the back garden.

"There isn't one because it's not actually a kitchen although it would have been once upon a time. The kitchen sink's through here." Dilly opened another lime green door. Beyond it were three steep, stone steps, "This is the actual kitchen. It's not as old as the rest of the house and is built of bricks rather than granite. It must have been added during an ancient modernisation plan. These steps would have originally led up to the back door which of course has long been replaced by the interior door."

"I see. I think," with a frown Freddie pointed to the corner of the rectangular room. "It's still quite old though, this kitchen, that is, because it even has a built-in copper."

Next to the brick built copper was a shallow ceramic sink. Khaki in colour with a solitary cold tap. To its left was a wooden draining board and next to that stood a table with a plastic tablecloth, very reminiscent of the nineteen fifties.

"Are there no modern appliances here?" Freddie ran his hands over a mangle on the table top beneath a small casement window.

"Of course," tutted Dilly, "There's a fridge in the cupboard under the stairs and you must have seen the telly on the sideboard, although I shall replace it with my own."

Before going out into the back garden they returned to the hallway where they had entered the house and climbed the stairs to the upper floor. To the left was a brown door and to the right a small landing. The brown door led into a large bedroom with dual aspect to the front and rear of the house. A double bed with varnished wood head and foot boards dominated the room. A matching wardrobe was nestled in an alcove and a tallboy and dressing table of similar style to the bed and wardrobe, stood around the edges of the irregular shaped room. Situated on either side of the bed were identical Windsor style chairs.

"This will be my room," enthused Dilly, "I love the fact that when I wake I'll be able to see the sea and my back garden as well but not in the same glance of course."

Freddie looked out of the back window. "Looks like you have an outside loo. That'll come in handy when you're out gardening."

Dilly chuckled. "It'll come in handy more often than that. It's the only one, you see, and although it's on mains drainage it doesn't have a flush so I suppose I'll have to carry buckets of water from the kitchen."

Freddie's jaw dropped.

Before he could comment, Amelia spoke, "Bert, and his parents before him, used to fill a bucket from the water butt outside the back door. When it had water in it, that is. During a dry summer it soon gets empty."

"So what's along the landing then?" Freddie asked.

"Two more bedrooms. Come and see." Dilly led the way. A door on the right of the landing led into a small empty room, its sloping floor covered with ancient cracked lino. On the opening side of its window were two vertical iron bars.

"Surely this wasn't used as a sort of prison." Freddie was horrified by the notion.

"No, no silly," laughed Amelia, "I commented on the bars once to Bert because you can see them from the front garden and he said his grandparents had them put in to stop his aunt, who had this room, from falling out when she was a little girl. It's a sheer drop onto the path below, you see."

"What happened to the aunt?" asked Freddie, "I mean if Bert's dad had a sister and maybe other siblings then Bert must have relations somewhere."

"I don't know because Bert was reluctant to talk about his family. But Ernie, who likes to chat when he goes to the pub, knows a bloke called John something or other who's into local history and he told Ernie that Bert's father, Frank, was knocked down and killed in a hit and run. They never found out who was responsible and it was even suggested it might have been deliberate. But whatever, the shock was too much for Bert's mum and she died following a heart attack a few days later."

"When was this?" Dilly asked.

"Not sure but I think it was in the nineteen-seventies. Ernie will remember better than me and in due course you'll no doubt get to meet John the historian I mentioned. If I remember correctly he was a fisherman before he retired."

"I shall look forward to that. It's always nice to know something of the people amongst whose ghosts you live."

Freddie shuddered. "Don't say that. It gives me the creeps."

Dilly laughed. "Come on. Let's finish the tour of the house."

The last room looked out over the back garden. By the window stood a dressing table and in an alcove a free standing wardrobe. The double bed was large, black and iron framed and on either side of it were chairs identical to those in Dilly's room.

"So, you're not kidding then. You have no bathroom and that is your only loo." Freddie pointed to the small building at the bottom of the garden.

"Well I did say the place needed a bit of plumbing work."

"A bit!" Freddie sat down on the window seat, "So what will you do? In fact what did Bert do when he wanted a bath?"

"I'll show you." Chuckling and chortling, Dilly led the way back down the stairs and into the front room. She crossed the threadbare carpet to where a thick, heavy brown curtain concealed an alcove. "Look in here," She pulled back the curtain to reveal an area the size of a very small room stacked with miscellaneous objects. Hanging on the back wall was a large tin bath.

"How about coming back to my place for a nice cup of tea?" said Amelia, noticing the lack of colour in Freddie's cheeks, "I've freshly made scones too, homemade strawberry jam and of course delicious Cornish clotted cream."

Dilly licked her lips. "Hmm, sounds delightful."

Freddie shook himself in an attempt to regain his composure. "I think I need something after seeing this house. I might even need to lie down in a darkened room."

Dilly punched his arm. "Oh, come on, Freddie it's not that bad. When I were a gel lots of houses were like this."

"I daresay they were but we're in the twenty-first century now and you're hardly in the first flush of youth to oversee all that needs doing in here to make it habitable. And I emphasise *all*."

"Nonsense, it'll be fun and I have my new friend Amelia here to guide me."

"Well I hope Amelia here knows some decent tradespeople."

"Don't worry, Freddie, I do. Ernie and I know several who are not only decent but reliable too."

Dilly smiled sweetly. "Anyway, what do you think of the place, Freddie? Not so much as it is now but from the point of view of its potential."

"Well I have to admit it has charm. It also has character and the location is stunning."

"That's what I wanted to hear because one day this will be all yours, Freddie."

They left Lavender Cottage via the back door and stopped to admire sweetly scented honeysuckle growing on the wall of a lean-to shed alongside the aforementioned water butt. Delighted by its perfume, Dilly tweaked off a flower and tucked its stem behind the brooch she wore on the lapel of her jacket.

"What are those funny things?" Freddie pointed towards a flower bed in front of a part tumbledown brick wall.

"Seed heads of honesty flowers," said Dilly, "often referred to as silver pennies."

"And very popular with flower arrangers," added Amelia.

They left the back garden through a small gate and walked along a path which led past the back of the enclosed entry and on to Amelia's house where they entered through the back door leading into the kitchen. Dilly and Freddie were instantly struck by the bright, airy warm room; a complete contrast to Lavender Cottage.

"Ah, this is more like it," Freddie looked around with approval.

"And mine will be similar one day. You wait and see." Dilly took a seat at the table after Amelia pulled out a chair for her. Freddie sat down opposite while Amelia filled the kettle.

"Your husband not here today?" Dilly asked.

"No, he's out fishing with his mates," Amelia looked at the clock, "should be back soon though as it's nearly high tide."

"Your husband is retired, I take it," said Freddie.

"That's right. He worked on the railway from the day he left school until he retired ten years ago. That's when we moved here."

"What did he do on the railway?"

Amelia took a tin from the top of the fridge containing the scones which she removed and laid out on a plate. "All sorts and then eventually he became a train driver. A fulfilled ambition held since he was in short trousers."

"Very nice and I suppose when he started the trains were all steam."

"They were indeed but he wasn't a driver back then. He's driven a fair amount of diesels though, and were he a bit younger and still working he'd have got to drive electric ones too. Although not very much because the lines are only electrified on our route between Paddington and Newbury so for most of the journey the bio-mode trains will be running on diesel and I doubt the rest of the line will be done anytime soon." Amelia made tea in a pot and placed it on the table along with the plate of scones, a dish of jam and a tub of cream. "Please help yourselves while I pour the tea."

"Thank you," said Dilly, "it all looks delicious."

"Yes, thank you," Freddie placed a scone on his plate and sliced it in two, "I was just thinking about Lavender Cottage and wonder why if Bert was a builder he never modernised the place himself."

"We've often pondered that," Amelia sat down, "Apparently he did the work to this place and so it seems odd that he didn't bother doing up his own house. Not you understand that we were around when the work was done here. It was like this when we bought it."

"Perhaps he liked his place as it was because it reminded him of his childhood," reasoned Dilly.

"Could well be," agreed Amelia. "As it is though we'll never know."

Freddie spread a layer of jam on the base of his scone. "So where did you live before you moved here?"

"Penzance and that's where Ernie and I met. I was down on holiday and we met at Demelza's, a nightclub which has been gone many a year."

"So you're not Cornish then?"

"No. Ernie is but I'm not. I've been here just over fifty years now though, so that's a big chunk of my life."

After they had finished their tea, Freddie stood up. "We really ought to get the stuff unloaded. I'd like to be home before midnight as I have work tomorrow and I need to return the hired van before I go in."

Dilly looked at her watch. "Yes, we ought to get a move on because I want to see if they can put me up in the pub for a few days until I get a bit straight. I had planned to stay next door tonight but it struck me as chilly in there so I think I'll treat myself to a bit of warmth."

Amelia picked up the empty mugs and placed them on the draining board. "You know you'd be more than welcome to stay with us, Dilly. We have two spare rooms and were you here you'd be on the spot to meet up with tradespeople and so forth."

"Oh, no, no. I can't put you to that much trouble. It wouldn't be fair on your husband."

"Ernie won't mind a bit. In fact he'll probably be quite glad because he'll be able to pop to the pub without feeling guilty about leaving me on my own."

Dilly hesitated. "Are you sure? It would only be for a couple of days, because once the old Truburn is going I'll have heat and I'll be able to rough it and then get things done gradually."

"And even then you must come here whenever you want a bath or a shower."

Dilly gave Amelia a hug. "Thank you so much."

"No, thank *you*. I'm thrilled to bits that you're our new neighbour and I'm sure you and I are going to be the best of friends."

Chapter Two

Freddie left the village just after six o'clock for the drive home, leaving his godmother to settle into Amelia and Ernie's largest guest room. Having recovered from the initial shock of seeing Lavender Cottage and its lack of amenities, calmness had overcome anxiety and he truly hoped she would enjoy her new life in Cornwall and that her new friend Amelia would prove to be great company for her.

His godmother had never married but had lived a fulfilling life. Until she had retired ten years earlier at the age of sixty-two, she had been a very active gym mistress at a girl's school. Following her retirement she continued to exercise daily and in the autumn of her years weighed much the same as she had done all her adult life. Freddie chuckled; her slight figure was a complete contrast to that of Amelia who stood just a few inches short of six feet and with a deep, commanding voice, typified the image he'd had as a boy of a sergeant major.

After just a few hours' sleep, Freddie left his flat the following morning, dropped off the hired vehicle and picked up his van; he then drove to his place of work wondering how his godmother was spending the first day of her new life in Cornwall.

In Cornwall, Dilly followed her exercise routine, took a shower and then went down to breakfast where Amelia was in the kitchen making scrambled eggs.

"Ah, there you are. I heard the shower so guessed you'd be down soon and before I forget to ask, did Freddie get home alright?"

"Yes, he rang me last night just as I was getting into bed."

"Jolly good. Lovely young man. Pity he couldn't stay a bit longer."

"I agree and I was sorry to see him go. Poor lamb, life has not treated him well."

Amelia turned away from the cooker. "Really? In what way?"

"In all sorts of ways going back quite a few years. He's one of two children and his older brother is called Luke. They're chalk and cheese and have never really seen eye to eye. Their parents split up when Freddie was twelve because their father took up with a younger woman and the pair eventually emigrated to her native land, Australia. Their mother soldiered on, took two jobs, struggled to pay the rent and died a few years later. Freddie likes to think it was of a broken heart. Perhaps it was but she was a heavy smoker and it took its toll. After she died the two brothers took over the rent and a few years later Freddie met Stacy. She was a solicitor and had her own place, so he left the family home he shared with his brother, glad to do so because Luke's girlfriend was in the throes of moving in. However, Freddie's relationship with Stacy didn't work out and after five years he left and now rents a small furnished flat above a fish and chip shop."

Amelia divided the scrambled eggs and placed a portion each on buttered toast. After putting one plate down in front of Dilly, she sat down with her own.

"But that's dreadful. Poor Freddie. So what does he do? Workwise, I mean."

"He's a plasterer. Works for one of the big building firms. Can't remember which."

"Building new homes?"

"Yes, I believe so."

"And the brother? What does he do?"

"He's an accountant's clerk. Something like that."

"And I take it you're not godmother to him."

"No, Luke's godmother is someone their dad used to work with. I can't remember her name but she was quite nice and I believe she and Luke are still in touch."

The back door opened and Ernie walked in with Oscar, his golden retriever.

"Morning ladies." While Oscar lapped up water from his bowl, Ernie removed the lead from his collar and hung it on the back of the door. "Bit nippy out there this morning but I reckon it's going to be a lovely day."

Amelia pointed towards a work surface. "There's tea in the pot if you'd like something to warm you up."

"Thanks love." Ernie removed his jacket and hung it on the door over the dog's lead. He then poured himself a mug of tea and sat down at the table. "I saw Dotty while I was out. She was resting on one of the benches along the seafront." He took a sip of tea. "Her face lit up when she saw me and she asked if someone had moved into Lavender Cottage because she saw the van outside yesterday. I told her yes and no, then explained the new owner was staying with us for a few days."

Amelia tutted. "Well, Dilly, your name will be known all round the village by lunchtime. Dotty is our resident writer, jogger, blogger and gossip. We reckon she must have binoculars or telescopes by every window in her house because she doesn't miss a trick."

"Actually, Dilly's name won't be all round the village yet because I didn't tell Dotty what it was. Silly woman was so excited by the prospect of a new inhabitant here she forgot to ask and I didn't say."

"So where does this Dotty live?" Dilly asked. "I mean, it must be in a good position if she's able to watch what's going on everywhere."

Amelia pointed towards the back of their house. "Up the hill at the top of the village in Short Lane. She has a good vantage point there and can see over most of the village."

"I see and you say she's a writer, jogger, blogger."

"And gossip," Amelia smiled, "She's actually very nice. She writes novels, blogs about fitness and health and jogs to keep fit."

"And also jogs so she can keep an eye on village activity." Ernie chuckled, "she was really impressed when I told her you're a retired gym mistress. In fact that's probably why she forgot to ask your name."

"What sort of age?" Dilly asked.

Amelia wrinkled her nose. "Early forties, possibly late thirties. Not really sure."

"She's forty," said Ernie, "Remember, she had a big bash at the pub earlier this year to celebrate. That is to say the event turned into being a big bash. You see, Dilly, Dotty just went in for a quiet meal with Gerry and a few friends but when the locals got wind of it they turned it into a full-blown party." He chuckled, "They're like that. The regulars at the Duck and Parrot. Any excuse for a knees-up."

"Oh dear, yes you're right. I remember now. We'd popped in for a quiet drink because there was nothing on the telly and got swept up by the occasion."

"I assume Gerry's her boyfriend or husband maybe."

"Boyfriend," said Amelia, "and he's a police sergeant. I think Dotty might have been married before at some point but can't remember for sure."

Ernie poured himself a second mug of tea. "She was married but she's divorced now. Remember, love, she's the one who was married to a minor television presenter and received a tidy sum from the divorce settlement which enabled her to buy a place here outright."

"That's right, yes, but of course it was before we knew her," Amelia watched her husband stir a spoonful of sugar into his tea and then turned to address Dilly. "It's just a thought, and please don't think I'm interfering, but Ernie saying about Dotty's failed marriage reminded me of Freddie and his relationship with the solicitor that went sour, and I wonder, if he's none too happy with his life and lives in a rented flat, then might it not be a good idea for you to offer him a home down here? I mean, if he's a plasterer he'd have no trouble finding work. He could even go self-employed and a lot of tradesmen down here prefer that. He'd be able to help do your place up as well and it'd give him a new lease of life. This is a very friendly village and I'm sure he'd settle in well."

Dilly finished off her last mouthful of scrambled egg and then laid down her knife and fork. "It's a lovely idea and I'd love to have him here but do you think he'd want to come? I mean, would a forty-six year old want to live with his old godmother?"

"Well there's only one way to find out. Ask him but make it clear you'll not be offended if he turns the offer down. But I'm sure he'd jump at the chance. I got the feeling he was reluctant to leave here yesterday despite the shock of seeing your place with its lack of facilities."

Ernie nodded. "I got the same impression and he seemed really interested when I got home with half a dozen mackerel as you were unloading your stuff. He listened to every word I said about my day out fishing and I think it really took his fancy."

"Yes," Dilly acknowledged, "I noticed how keen he seemed."

"Why not give him a ring? Strike while the iron is hot." Amelia stood up, collected the dirty plates and opened the door of the dishwasher.

"I won't ring now because he'll be at work. In fact I won't ring at all. I'll pop next door and send an email, that way I can put forward my case and it'll give him time to think before he responds."

"That's a good idea," smiled Amelia, "but you'll have to bring your laptop round here if you do because you don't have the internet yet."

"Bother. I'd not thought of that even though it's one of my priority things to do today." Amelia leaned back in her chair, "Actually, it won't be necessary though because I'm going to do it the good old fashioned way and send a letter by post."

"But an email will be so much quicker," reasoned Amelia.

"It will. I agree. But it also means he'll receive it on his phone while at work and I'd much rather he read it when he got home."

"Very good point," agreed Amelia, "and I'm sure when he gets home and reads it it'll make his day."

"I hope so. I really do."

At half past five on a Friday afternoon, two days after Dilly had written the letter, Freddie arrived home from work and parked his van alongside the kerb opposite the fish and chip shop. It was the weekend, he felt grubby and was tired. Too tired even to go to the pub. Because he wasn't in the mood for cooking, he planned to enjoy a cold beer in front of the television, watch a film maybe and then order a takeaway later. He wasn't sure whether he fancied, Chinese, Indian or pizza. He could even pop down below and get fish and chips, but whatever, he'd decide after he'd had a chance to put his feet up and relax.

When he stepped inside the flat he picked up the post without looking at it. Most of it appeared to be junk mail and so he dropped it along with his lunchbox on the kitchen worktop and then went for a leisurely shower. He felt a lot better once clean and wearing a change of clothes. With a little more energy, he took a can of beer from the fridge and a packet of crisps from a cupboard and carried both along with the post into his small sitting room. He opened the bag of crisps, popped a few into his mouth and then shuffled through the post. When he saw the white envelope with a handwritten address tucked amongst colourful advertising leaflets, he was surprised, for like many, he'd not received a handwritten letter for as long as he could remember. Curious as to who it might be from, he dropped the junk mail onto the floor and tore the envelope open. When he saw the address at the top of the page his jaw dropped. When he read the letter his heart rate increased. Thinking he must have read it wrong, he read it again. Feeling in need of air he crossed the room and opened the window. The smell of fish and chips wafted up from the shop below and any view he might have had was blocked by the row of houses opposite. He took in a deep breath and looked up to the heavens where the outline of a new moon was just visible in the slowly darkening sky. If he did as his godmother suggested the outlook from his home would not be a row of houses but an uninterrupted view of the sea. He could go fishing and catch mackerel with Ernie and Ernie's friends. Become a self-employed tradesman. Help do up Lavender Cottage. Begin a new chapter in his life. He could even have a bath in the old tin bath. There really was nothing to lose. With a huge grin on his face, he closed the window, picked up his mobile phone and selected his godmother's number.

Chapter Three

With very few possessions to his name, Freddie knew moving would not need a great deal of planning, and the following day he gave notice to his employer and to his landlord. He then advertised the few things he'd have no further need of on social media and made a list of jobs to complete before his departure. Two weeks later he went out for a farewell meal with Luke and Luke's girlfriend, Louise. Luke wished his younger brother the best of luck with his new venture and they promised to keep in touch. The following day Freddie put the last of his possessions inside his van, posted the keys to the flat through the letterbox and set off for Cornwall.

The September sun was setting when he arrived at Lavender Cottage where his godmother and Amelia sat in the living room by the Truburn waiting for him. On the dining table in the centre of the room, a bottle of wine and three glasses stood ready to celebrate his safe arrival.

He parked at the side of the house where his godmother proposed to have a garage built even though she had no vehicle due to its MOT failure and had no plans to replace it.

Having heard his van park outside, the front door of the house was opened before Freddie had a chance to knock. As he stepped into the hall, he hugged his godmother and kissed her on the cheek. She then led him into the living room where overcome by the occasion he also hugged Amelia who had risen to her feet to greet him.

"I must say, this room looks and feels a whole lot different now the fire is lit." He looked approvingly at the open door of the Truburn where warmth emanated from the glowing coke behind the grid, "It smells sweeter too."

"It does," agreed Dilly, "It's surprising the difference being lived in makes to a place."

Freddie removed his jacket and looked around for somewhere to put it.

"Hang it on the pegs in the hall," said Dilly, as she poured three glasses of wine.

Freddie opened the door, hung up his coat and returned to the room grinning. "I see you've yet to dispose of Bert's old coats."

"Not only Bert's but there are ladies garments too which I assume must have belonged to his mother and probably even his grandmother."

Freddie took the proffered glass of wine, clinked it with the ladies and then sat down in one of the three armchairs. "So what do you propose to do with the old coats and the rest of Bert's things?"

"I don't know and that's why they're still there. It seems wrong to throw them away but at the same time I know they'll have to go at some point."

"Well, I suppose there's no rush. Anyway, what have you done so far? Other than pick dahlias and put them in vases. Which look very nice I might add."

"Not a lot. Mostly cleaning and so forth."

"And you had the chimney swept and the internet installed," Amelia reminded her.

"That's right I did. I've also had a delivery of coke. It's in the little lean-to outbuilding, which has a leaky roof I've discovered. Oh yes, and another thing, I've had my washing machine plumbed in. It's only a temporary measure until we get a proper kitchen built but it's fine for now."

"So apart from having a new kitchen and a bathroom at some point, have you any other improvement plans in the pipeline?"

Dilly shook her head. "Other than expose the fireplace in this room, no, and that must wait 'til next summer because the Truburn is our only source of heat. As regards the rest of the house, I thought I'd wait until you were here to see what you think. Also, Ernie said not to rush in and do something I might regret and I can see his point. So if you're in agreement we can probably live in it as it is now for the winter and make any drastic changes next year."

"Sounds good to me," said Freddie.

"And Ernie and I insist you make use of our bathroom so personal hygiene won't be a problem."

Dilly smiled. "And we're grateful for that. As for the loo, it's surprising how one gets used to carrying a bucket of water down the garden path."

"Even in the rain?" Freddie chuckled.

"Yes, even in the rain."

Over the next few days, Freddie settled in. His room was the second largest with the double iron framed bed and a view over the lean-to shed and the back garden. Dilly suggested the small room next to it which faced the sea be his too so that he could sit on the window seat in there should he wish to do so. She even offered to get the iron rods, installed to prevent Bert's aunt, when a child, from falling out, removed, but Freddie felt they must stay as they were a part of the house's history. Because the house had no heating other than the Truburn, Freddie and Dilly went shopping and bought hot water bottles and electric heaters for their bedrooms. There was already one at the house but both agreed safety was the essence and it would be foolhardy to use an electric fire that was probably older than Freddie.

"I reckon this house was originally two and they, no doubt the Brays, knocked both into one," said Freddie when he came in from the lean-to shed where he had filled the scuttle with coke.

"Most likely. Amelia said their place was originally two so it stands to reason it might be the same here but what makes you say that?"

"Come and see."

Freddie led Dilly back out to the lean-to, "Look in the back wall. Part of it is brick and I think there was originally a door there which would have led into the front room."

Dilly stepped forwards and examined the wall blackened by years of storing coke. "You're right, and that means this would be the ideal place to access a bathroom extension. I'd wondered how it could be done and this is the answer. We can knock down the kitchen and this lean-to and have a single storey bathroom, kitchen and passage extension running along the entire length of the house with access from the front room and the living room."

"Sounds great. Might even be a worth considering having an upstairs loo installed by the small window on the landing."

"Oh, absolutely. I'll get an architect round to see what he thinks because it'll take a while to gets plans drawn up, approved and all the rest of it."

"Do you know one? Architect, that is."

"No, but Ernie does and he says the two of them often have a game of pool at the pub. He's a frequent visitor there, you see. The architect, that is, because he lives in a nice house just a stone's throw away from it."

"Talking of which. I think it's time we went to the pub. You and Amelia often mention it but I've yet to see it, let alone pay it a visit."

"In which case we'll go this evening and I'll see if Amelia and Ernie will join us and then if the architect's there, Ernie can introduce us."

The Duck and Parrot, a large granite-built freehouse fondly known by the locals as the Duck, lay further along the village overlooking the sea with views similar to those of Lavender Cottage. As well as having two bars and a dining room, it had a well-equipped games room, a purpose built smoking area and four letting rooms. The licensees, Gail and Robert Stevens, a married couple in their mid-fifties, had been in the pub for just over four years and due to their easy-going nature were very popular with the locals and holiday makers alike.

Because the evening was dry and the south-westerly wind little more than a gentle breeze, Dilly, Freddie, Amelia and Ernie walked the short distance to the pub to enable each of them to enjoy an alcoholic drink or two. As they ambled along the paved seafront towards their destination, all traces of an earlier golden sunset had vanished and a near-full moon was visible in the slowly darkening sky.

After buying drinks, they sat at a table in the corner and Ernie pointed out a few people who he considered might of interest to the newcomers. "That bloke sitting at the bar drinking Guinness is Denzil Williams, he's a builder who lives here in the village and I've heard he's very good. The older chap next to him wearing the red shirt is John Martin, he's a retired fisherman and a historian and the chap to go to if you want to know anything of the village's history. The good-looking chap standing over by the fruit machine is Gerry Freeman. He's the copper boyfriend of Dotty, the jogger blogger. Unfortunately, the very person I wanted you to meet, Julian Patterson the architect, isn't here which is typical."

"Damn! That means we'll have to come again another night," the glint in Freddie's eyes underlined his delight at the prospect.

"That sounds a good idea but there's no rush anyway," said Dilly, "Meanwhile, at some point I'd like to get to know the historian chap and learn a little more about Bert's family, and the village of course."

"Without doubt, John's the chap for that. I'd call him over now but he seems to be deep in conversation with Denzil."

A little later, John the historian left and shortly after, Denzil drained his glass and said goodbye to landlord, Robert. Doing up the zip of his jacket as he headed for the door he caught Dilly's eye. "You wouldn't by any chance be the new owner of Lavender Cottage, would you? It's just I saw you picking flowers in the front garden the other day. At least I think it was you."

"Yes I am and it was me." She smiled sweetly thrilled to have been recognised.

He offered his hand. "Then pleased to meet you. The name's Denzil Williams."

Dilly shook the proffered hand. "Likewise, and I'm Dilly Granger. Ernie tells me you're a builder so I may well call on your services at some point."

"I'd be delighted. Smashing looking place you have and one of the oldest buildings in the village."

"Thank you. I guessed it was pretty old and I like it more every day."

Denzil cast a puzzled look at Freddie. "Would this be your son, Dilly? It's just someone said something about a younger relative living with you."

Freddie raised his hand. "Nearly right, but I'm Dilly's godson, not son. Freddie Hewitt's the name."

Denzil shook Freddie's hand. "I see, and would I be right in thinking you're a plasterer?"

"My goodness word does travel fast. Yes, I am and I have all the bits of paper to back up the fact. I used to work for property developers but intend to go self-employed down here."

"That's music to my ears, so when you're up and ready I'll be able to put plenty of work your way. The chap I used to use retired recently so I've been a bit stuck without him."

"Well, that's brilliant and I can be ready whenever you are. I already have a van, so just need to get a few tools together and register with HMRC as self-employed."

"Great. If you let me have your number then I'll be in touch."

"We were hoping to see Julian Patterson this evening," said Ernie, as phone numbers were exchanged.

"Well, he won't be in tonight because he and the missus have gone away for a couple of days to celebrate their thirtieth wedding anniversary or something like that. Should be back sometime tomorrow though. I've got his number if you'd like it."

"Wonderful," gushed Dilly, "that will be very useful."

"Well, I'm really glad we came," said Freddie, as Denzil left the pub. "He seems like a nice bloke."

"Everyone seems nice," said Dilly. "Luck was definitely on my side when I found Lavender Cottage."

The following morning, Freddie drove his van to the builders' merchants where he opened an account and bought the necessary tools and equipment required for plastering. When he returned to Lavender Cottage he registered on-line with HMRC.

"Cup of tea?" Dilly asked, as he closed down the laptop.

"Yes please."

Dilly took two mugs from the kitchen cabinet, dropped a teabag in each and then poured on boiling water from one of the two kettles on top of the Truburn.

"I must admit," said Freddie, as she handed him his tea, "I'm rather liking this primitive way of life. There's something satisfying about living without all the mod cons. Admittedly we have the internet, mobile phones, coloured telly and so forth but it's still possible with having just one cold tap, and a loo at the bottom of the garden with no flush, to get the feel of life in days-gone-by."

Dilly sat down. "I'm really pleased to hear that because I feel much the same and I don't know about you but I think we'll leave the main part of the house pretty much as it is now. I'm not even sure about exposing the fireplace because this old stove is really efficient and it'll be a godsend come the colder weather. It's just a shame it doesn't heat the rest of the house."

"You could always get a log burner in the fireplace once it's exposed and some even have cooking facilities. I think it would look great."

"You're right but for now we'll leave any plans for change until after the extension's done and central heating is installed. Which reminds me, I rang Julian Patterson the architect this morning while you were at the builders' merchants and he's popping round to see us tomorrow morning around elevenish."

"Ideal," Freddie glanced at the old mantel clock on the sideboard. "Would you think me daft if I said I'm thinking of having a bath in the old tin tub? Just to see what it's like."

Dilly laughed and then realised he was speaking in earnest. "Well if you do for the sake of modesty I'd better make myself scarce."

"It won't be for a while yet and I think rather than go to the trouble of lighting the copper I'll fill the Baby Burco. Assuming it works, that is."

"It does. I put some water in to try it out so I could do some washing while I waited for my automatic to be plumbed in."

"Good. I'll fill it up shortly then and plan to have a bath around seven o'clock."

Just before seven as the water in the Baby Burco came to the boil, Dilly slipped on her shoes. She had offered to help Freddie prepare his bath but he said he wanted to do it himself to see just how much hardship was involved and he'd faithfully report his experience to her when she returned from a visit to see Amelia and Ernie who were amused by Freddie's plans.

Removing the bath tub from its nail behind the curtain was straightforward. Likewise, placing it on the rug in front of the Truburn was simple and so was filling it with buckets of hot water from the boiler. But Freddie conceded that taking water from the old copper would be far more laborious as there was no tap and so water would need to be scooped out.

Once the bath was half full and with cold water added to achieve an acceptable temperature, Freddie removed his clothing and stepped into the bath. For a little comfort he reached behind to the armchair and pulled off a cushion and placed it behind his head. Leaning back he grinned to himself. It was all quite pleasant although he felt rather exposed bathing in a spacious room and wondered how large families had coped in days gone by. Freddie looked to the clock on the sideboard when it struck the half hour. His eyes then drifted to a framed photograph of two men alongside a truck bearing the name Frank Bray & Son, Builders. He assumed the two men were Bert and his father, Frank, and recalled Amelia telling them that Frank was killed in a hit and run which might have been deliberate but the driver was never found. Freddie pondered over their plight until the water cooled. He then reached for a towel and stepped out onto the rug.

Dilly returned to the house after Freddie sent her a text saying he was decent and in the throes of emptying the bath tub. He was tipping the last bucket down the sink when she walked in through the back door.

"How did it go?"

"Fine but it's very time consuming and after emptying it I don't feel very refreshed. In fact quite the opposite."

Dilly picked up an old cloth. "I'll wipe the bath out and hang it back up and you go and put your feet up."

Once the bath was back behind the curtain from where it was unlikely to see the light of day again for a very long time, Dilly poured them both a glass of Shiraz and sat down in the chair opposite her godson.

"Thank you," Freddie took several gulps of wine and then stood the glass on the floor by his feet. "I was thinking about the Brays while I was in the tub and you'll probably think me daft but I've got a bee in my bonnet about what happened to Bert's dad. I mean, we know it was a hit and run that killed him, but was it deliberate? And if it wasn't, why did the driver not stop? No doubt the case has long been put to rest but I can't help but wonder and I think I want to try and find out what happened; and if it was deliberate, what was the motive behind it."

"That sounds rather exciting and it'd be a worthwhile project with the coming winter nights, so if you want a helping hand, count me in."

"Brilliant. We'll start tomorrow then although I'm not sure how to go about it."

"By asking questions, I suppose and looking for clues amongst Bert's stuff. Family birth certificates might be here somewhere. Death certificates too even. If so it'd be interesting to see what they say and it'll help us get a picture of the family and the lives they each led."

Chapter Four

The next morning, the architect called and they discussed possible ways of installing or adding a bathroom and a modern kitchen. They could either demolish the old brick-built kitchen and convert the current living room and have a bathroom upstairs, or demolish the old brick kitchen and the lean-to shed and have a brand new extension built but that would mean losing part of the garden. Dilly was unsure and conceded that perhaps they had not been in the house long enough to get the feel of the place. Julien agreed and suggested, as had Ernie, that if they could manage as things were, then it would be best to leave a decision until the New Year when they were more familiar with the place.

After the architect left they began to search through the two cupboards and four drawers in the sideboard looking for any information regarding the Bray family. Dilly already knew the top drawer contained cutlery because she had put in her own alongside it. The next two drawers contained papers and the bottom a selection of hats, scarves and gloves. They each pulled out a drawer of papers and sat on the floor to go through the contents. Dilly found nothing other than utility bills going back over many years, maps of Cornwall and manuals for household appliances. Freddie, however, was more successful, for at the bottom of his drawer, along with war-time identity cards, medical cards and Bert's driving licence, he found a large envelope with 'certificates' written in bold print across the front.

"Aha, bingo." Freddie stood up, carefully opened the envelope and laid out its contents on the table. He then pulled out a chair and sat down to see what he had found.

Dilly, glad to get up for she had pins and needles in her legs from sitting on the floor, sat down next to him. "This is just what we need and should give us some idea of Bray family members and so forth."

After sorting through the certificates and getting them in order they established that Bert, down as Albert, was born in 1935. They already knew he had no siblings but were pleased to learn that his parents were Francis Bray born in 1912 and Ethel Bray, nee Rowe, born in 1913. They were married in 1931 at St. Stephen's Church in Trenwalloe Sands. Their death certificates were also present and confirmed that in 1975 Francis died from injuries sustained in a road traffic accident and that Ethel died from heart failure a few days later.

"So far so good," Dilly pushed the read certificates to one side, "now let's see if we can discover who these other bits of paper refer to."

Francis's parents were George Bray born in 1880 and his mother was Elizabeth Bray, nee Jago, born in 1885. George died in 1945 and Elizabeth in 1940. After studying further they established that Francis, known as Frank, must have had a brother named Eric because they found a telegram from the war office informing his father George that Eric was lost, presumed dead, in 1942.

"Oh, that's so sad," sighed Dilly, "poor Eric."

"It is sad and perhaps a blessing that his mother predeceased him and so never learned of his death." As Freddie put the telegram to one side he spotted another birth certificate, "Aha, this is for Eric and he was born in 1914 meaning he was just twenty-eight when he died."

"So it looks as though Frank had just the one brother, Eric," said Dilly, "who as we've just established died during the Second World War."

"As it seems did his parents," said Freddie, "if they died in 1940 and 1945."

"Meaning, it must have been in 1945, after George's demise that Frank and his wife Ethel moved here to Lavender Cottage along with their son, Albert of course, who would have then been ten at that time."

Freddie frowned. "It's just occurred to me, but why didn't Frank go to war? I mean, builders weren't exempt from conscription, were they?"

"No, so perhaps he had a disability of some sort or health problems even."

"Must have been something like that but it doesn't really matter anyway as far as our enquiries go. Even though it's Frank's dubious death we're looking into."

Dilly gathered up the certificates. "We haven't really learned a great deal, have we?"

"No, but we know more than we did. The most significant thing being Frank had just one sibling, Eric, who died during the war and had no issue. Hence Bert having no close family members to leave this house and his possessions to." Freddie picked up Bert's driving licence. "Meanwhile, better not put this back in the drawer. It needs returning to the DVLA so I'll do that along with a note explaining how come we have it."

"Of course. Must keep on the right side of the law," Dilly gathered up the birth, marriage and death certificates and placed them back in the envelope. As she dropped it inside the drawer, the back door opened. "Co-ee. Only me. Can I come in?"

"Of course, you're always welcome and just in time as I was about to ask Freddie if he'd like a cup of tea."

Freddie stood up. "I'll make it as I'm sure you'll want to tell Amelia what we've discovered."

"You've discovered something? How wonderful."

Amelia listened carefully and hung on to every word spoken. She then frowned. "But there had to be a sister as well. Remember what I told you about the bars at the window in your small bedroom."

Dilly frowned. "But weren't they to stop Bert falling out or something like that?"

"To stop someone falling out, yes, but not Bert. Bert said they were installed by his grandfather to stop his aunt falling out."

Dilly frowned. "Are you sure?"

"Absolutely, because when Bert told me my imagination conjured up the image of a curly haired little girl with freckles and a sad face as she held on to the bars."

"Which means," said Freddie, "that Frank and Eric must have had a sister."

"Unless it was an aunt on Frank's mother's side of the family," reasoned Dilly.

Freddie took three mugs from the kitchen cabinet. "No, can't be the case because she wouldn't have been a Bray and so wouldn't have lived here."

"So why haven't we come across her birth certificate?" Dilly was puzzled.

Amelia sat down at the table and gently drummed her fingers on the Formica top. "The most logical reason I would think is that she moved away. Married even, and took it with her."

"Damn," cursed Dilly, "of course that would be the case."

Freddie took one of the kettles from the Truburn. "So how do we find out who she was?"

"John, our historian," said Amelia, "He's bound to know."

"But surely he'll not be old enough," reasoned Dilly, "I mean, it must be nearly a hundred years since the sister was born and so probably sixty or seventy since she went away."

35

Amelia was adamant. "He'll know. He's an expert on families who have their roots well established here and if he doesn't know, well, he'll find out. He's great mates with the vicar, you see. They and a couple of others play bridge together, so John will be able to take a look at the church records as he's done on many occasions before."

"Sounds like this John is someone we must get to know," said Dilly.

Amelia nodded. "He is. I'll get Ernie to give him a ring and arrange for him to pop round and see you some time."

Amelia was as good as her word and the following morning she called round to say if it was okay with them John would call round the following evening, Friday. Meanwhile, he'd get together as much information as possible about the Brays so that hopefully he could answer any questions they might have.

No sooner had she left than Freddie received a call from Denzil Williams, the builder, offering him work commencing the following Monday along with himself and his team who were doing a barn conversion for farmer Max Pascoe. Max lived and worked at Hilltop Farm situated on the outskirts of the village.

"Wow! It's all happening today," Freddie glanced out the window, "and since it looks like I'll be working next week I think I better cut the grass while it's dry."

"Good idea and I'll pop out and cut a few more dahlias and tidy the plants up a bit. They're getting past their best now so I want to get some for indoors before they go over completely."

"Righto, and first one to finish makes the morning coffee."

Freddie went out of the back door, collected the electric lawnmower from the dry corner of the lean-to shed and to avoid it being knocked by the cable, he pushed to one side a tray of well rooted lavender cuttings taken by Bert shortly before his demise. Meanwhile, with scissors in hand, Dilly went out of the front door and into the garden. She contemplated gathering some of the yellow pompom chrysanthemums that grew alongside the green railings but decided against it as she didn't want to spoil the plants' bushy shapes. As she gathered a bunch of dahlias, a jogger slowed her pace and stopped.

"Please don't think me nosy but are you the gym mistress who owns this place. I've seen you around and so think you must be."

"Yes, I am and you must be Dotty the jogger blogger."

Dotty laughed. "Has someone been telling tales about me?"

"Only in a pleasant way. It was Ernie next door. The day after I moved here he mentioned he'd seen you and the phrase jogger blogger gelled with me. I believe you're a writer too." Dilly refrained from adding gossip to her statement.

"Ah, dear old Ernie, he's a nice chap and yes, I am a writer."

"What do you write?"

"Romantic fiction."

"Oh, I see. Not my cup of tea then."

"I don't know, you might be surprised. You're never too old for a bit of romance."

"Hmm, not sure about that. By the way, my name's Dilly."

"Dilly and Dotty. I like it." Dotty started running on the spot, "My real name is Dorothy but I couldn't say that when I was little and called myself Dotty. It was Dad who chose Dorothy because it was his mother's name. Mum on the other hand wanted to call me Sophia after her mother. In the end they tossed for it and Dad won."

"Well, that's one way of settling it, I suppose."

"Yes. Mum partly got her way though because Sophia is my middle name. Anyway, must get on but if you ever fancy a jog let me know as it's always nice to have someone to run with."

"Thank you. I might just do that." Dilly watched as Dotty jogged off, she then finished cutting flowers and removed a few dead leaves. When done she returned indoors, put the dahlias in vases and went out the back to see how Freddie was getting on.

"Done already?" she said, seeing him removing clumps of grass from the bottom of the mower.

"Yes, doesn't take long. Nice and flat with no awkward bits. Have you finished too?"

"Yes I have so I'll make the coffee."

"Before you go, come over here and look back at the kitchen."

Dilly did as she was asked. "What exactly am I looking at?"

Freddie raised his arm and pointed. "The position of the window."

Dilly frowned. "I can't see what you're getting at."

"When you're in the kitchen the window is in the middle of the wall, but when you look at it out here, it isn't."

"Oh, I see what you mean. There's definitely more wall to one side than the other."

"Exactly, and I reckon there must have been a pantry or something at the end and for some reason it's been bricked up."

"If that's the case it probably had a window and there might be evidence of it behind the jasmine."

"Good thinking." They both stepped towards the wall and started to pull away at the foliage where a window was most likely to have been.

"You're right," gasped Dilly, as their search revealed a small area of different coloured bricks.

Without another word spoken, both dashed into the kitchen and pulled away the Burco boiler and an old paraffin heater which stood in the corner. Freddie then tapped over the area where it was logical for a door to be situated.

"Sounds hollow, like it's a stud wall," Freddie stepped back, "There's no doubt about it, there would have been a doorway here."

"But why's it been blocked up?"

"Search me."

"Well I suppose there's only one way to find out."

"I was hoping you'd say that. I'll fetch some tools."

"And I'll fetch Amelia." Dilly dashed out the back door as Freddie went round the side of the house to his van for tools.

On their return, all three took items from the kitchen they were able to carry and put them outside onto the path to avoid plaster dust. Bulkier items they covered with old sheets. After closing the door into the living room and placing a towel along the gap at the bottom, Freddie then began to chip off chunks of plaster and drop the lumps into a large gorilla basket. Dilly and Amelia, huddled close together with arms linked, watched feeling both nervous and excited.

"What will we do if there's a body in there?" said Amelia.

Chuckling, Freddie stopped chipping and picked up pieces of plaster that had fallen onto the floor. "I can't see why there would be. I mean, as far as we know no-one is missing."

"Bert's aunt is," gushed Dilly.

The colour drained from Amelia's face. "No, I can't believe Bert would bump off his aunt and seal her up in a pantry. He always struck me as such a nice chap."

"It might not have been Bert. It could have been Frank. I mean, they were both builders weren't they?" Dilly bit at the nails on her free hand.

"What a couple of drama queens," laughed Freddie. "I expect it was bricked up because it had a leaking roof or something like that."

"Nonsense, if that were the case they'd have fixed it," retorted Dilly.

Freddie, thinking it best not to reply, continued chipping away at the plaster until he was able to see wood. "Well blow me. They must have plastered over the door. I'm surprised at builders doing a botched job like that."

Amelia gasped. "Probably done in a hurry then."

"Aha," said Freddie, "there's a small hole here where the latch would have been."

"Can you see through it?" Dilly asked.

"No, too dark in there."

Freddie continued chipping and to speed up the process the ladies picked up plaster that missed the basket. When the chocolate brown panelled door was finally clear they swept up the debris to allow it to open.

"Ready?" asked Freddie, as he slipped his finger into the hole and moved the door slightly.

"Ready," said the ladies in unison.

For dramatic effect, Freddie slowly pulled back the door and when fully open three heads peeped inside the dark area where, with the window bricked up, the only light was from the kitchen. As anticipated, it was a pantry. Cobwebs hung from the ceiling and two shelves ran the entire length of the wall opposite. On a thick slate beneath the bricked up widow, sat an old meat safe. Empty jars stood on the dirty floor along with old glass milk bottles and a broom with a broken handle. The rest of the floor was taken up by a dust covered Harley Davidson.

Chapter Five

"A bloomin' motorbike," Dilly was clearly disappointed.

"It looks a beauty though," enthused Amelia, "Ernie used to have a Harley in his younger days. He'll be fascinated by this."

"But why is it here?" Freddie approached the bike and picked up a crash helmet resting on the seat, "I mean, surely Bert didn't use the pantry to keep it in and even if he did, why shut it away?"

"No, he couldn't have housed it in here, his mum would surely never have allowed it," reasoned Amelia, "I mean, before everyone had fridges and freezers the pantry was an important part of the house."

Eager to establish how long it might have been hidden away, Dilly brushed dust from the bike's tax disc with her handkerchief. "Good heavens, 1975, so it must have been here ever since then otherwise the tax would have been renewed."

"I agree," said Amelia, "and my guess is that it belonged not to Bert but to his dad, Frank, and when Frank died I bet Bert sealed it up in the pantry for sentimental reasons rather than get rid of it. I mean, it's a fine looking machine and was most likely Frank's pride and joy."

"Good theory," agreed Freddie, "but how do we find out?"

"Once again, John, the historian," said Amelia, "because even if he doesn't know why it's here he should at least remember who used to ride it."

Freddie frowned. "What! Surely he'll not be able to remember after forty-seven years."

"Well, yes, I admit it is rather a long time ago but he's lived here all his life so I'm sure he'd have a memory of something like that."

"How old is he?" Dilly asked, "John that is."

"Not sure of his exact age but it's somewhere around the eighty mark."

"Hmm, so he'd have been in his mid-thirties when this was shut away. Quite possible that he'll remember then."

"I'm sure he will. Meanwhile, what are you going to do with it?" Amelia asked.

"Nothing 'til John's seen it," said Freddie, "Then I suppose we could get it out and clean it up. Might even be able to take it for a spin."

"Well, when it comes to that I'd get Ernie involved if I were you because what he doesn't know about Harleys isn't worth knowing."

"Is he home at the moment?" Freddie asked.

"Sadly not. He's gone blackberrying."

"Oh, well, never mind he can see it later because with two flat tyres it's going nowhere at the moment." Freddie closed the pantry door.

"Would you like me to vacuum the kitchen floor?" Amelia surveyed their footprints in the crumbled plaster.

"Later, and while you do I'll wipe down the filthy surfaces," Dilly leaned across the steps leading into the living room and removed the towel from the bottom of the door, "Meanwhile, let's have a cup of tea. I feel quite thirsty after breathing in all that dust."

As pre-arranged, John Martin called at Lavender Cottage the following evening. Amelia and Ernie were also there as both were keen to hear any information the historian might have as regards their erstwhile neighbour's family.

In his early eighties, John Martin was a tall man who looked fit and well for his age. This he put down to years of working in the fresh air, hauling crab-pots and lugging around boxes of fish. He retired shortly after his seventieth birthday. Not because he wanted to but because he thought safety might be an issue. For although he was a strong man he accepted his reactions had slowed over the years and he didn't want the lives of others to be at risk were he to do something stupid and need to be rescued. After selling his boat and fishing gear he found himself with time on his hands. Having never married and with no offspring to think of, he filled his days by furthering his knowledge of Trenwalloe Sands and its history. The more he discovered the more he enjoyed his new hobby and soon he was considered to be an expert on the subject.

Before the meeting commenced, Ernie enthusiastically took John to the pantry to show him the Harley Davidson and both men agreed it was a magnificent machine. All five then sat around the table in the living room to make it easier to show John the birth, marriage and death certificates and look at any papers or documents that he might have brought along, "Before we begin," said Dilly, "would anyone like a glass of wine? I bought two bottles today in anticipation."

All nodded and uttered words of thanks as their hostess placed two bottles, one red and the other white in the centre of the table and passed everyone a glass. "The white's been chilled as you can see by the condensation on the bottle, so please help yourselves."

With glasses filled all eyes turned to their guest. "We're ready when you are, John," said Ernie, "but goodness knows where you'll want to begin."

"Well I think the first thing ought to be the motorbike. Freddie told me your theory, Amelia: that it belonged to Frank and that Bert hid it away for sentimental reasons after Frank died, but that wasn't the case at all. Without doubt the bike belonged to Bert and as far as I know Frank never rode it. What's more, it certainly wouldn't have been housed in the pantry because I'm told Ethel was very house-proud. Furthermore, she didn't like it. Said it was a monstrosity and wasn't happy about it at all. I got this snippet of information from Bruce, my older brother, who worked with Frank and Bert for a while. I rang him when I heard about the bike, you see, and he remembers it well."

"So why on earth did Bert seal it up in the pantry?" Freddie asked.

"That I can't tell you but it certainly wouldn't have been while Ethel was alive."

"We reckon it must have been sometime in 1975," said Amelia, "because of the tax disc."

"And that's the year in which Bert's parents both died," Freddie added.

"Correct," said John, "Poor Frank was knocked down in a hit and run and Ethel died a few days later following a heart attack. But you no doubt know that already because I see you have their death certificates."

Freddie glanced at the two certificates. "That's right we do and the deaths seem quite straightforward albeit Frank's is unsolved and we'd like to look into that later. At the moment though what's bothering me is if the bike belonged to Bert, why on earth did he hide it away?"

John shook his head. "Sorry to say I've no idea."

"Might your brother know?" Amelia asked.

"No. He wasn't working with them then. You see, mackerel fishing was taking off and because there was big money to be made, I gave him a berth on my boat and that'd have been in 1974 and so the year before Frank, and then Ethel died. After that Bruce didn't see much of the Brays other than bumping into them in the pub. He knew the bike had gone though, but assumed Bert had sold it so that he could concentrate on the building business. I mean, with both his parents gone he suddenly had a lot more responsibility."

"He did, poor chap. It must have been a nightmare." Dilly cast a glance at the framed photograph on the sideboard of Bert and his father alongside their truck.

"So it looks likely it'll remain a mystery," said Amelia, "What a shame."

"I don't know; it's early days yet," said Dilly, "and I'm sure we'll find out more in due course. After all, faint heart never won fair lady." She turned to the historian. "I wonder if you can shed any light on something Bert said to Amelia, John. He made reference to an aunt who we assume was Frank's sister, but we can't find her birth certificate or any mention of her anywhere."

"You're right, Frank did have a sister and her name was Joan. She was born in 1918 the same year as my mother. Mum and Joan were at school together and were quite good friends in their early years. After that Joan became a bit of a handful and one night early in 1939 she had a blazing row with her parents. The next morning she packed her bags and left and they never heard from her again. As for her birth certificate, I expect she took it with her. It upset Elizabeth, her mum, badly. Some said it put her in an early grave. She died the following year, you see, and it didn't help that a few months after Joan left the War broke out."

"Oh dear," tutted Dilly, "What on earth can the argument have been about for her to have never got in touch again."

"According to Mum there was lots of speculation at the time but no-one knows for sure and I suppose after all these years we never will. It caused quite an upset though and as I said, some reckoned it sent Elizabeth to an early grave."

Dilly looked up at the picture of Elizabeth hanging above the television set. "Poor, poor lady. No wonder she has sad eyes. I wish I could have known her."

"You'd have liked her," said John, "Not that I knew her. But Mum did; back in the days when she and Joan were mates she often came here. I remember Mum telling me that Joan's mother was fascinating. She read tealeaves, you see, but more importantly she was a wonderful cook and always had a full cake tin. She added lavender to some of her buns and Mum said they were delicious."

"Ah cakes! That explains her umm…how shall I put it. I know, that explains her having a fuller figure."

"Freddie," scolded Dilly, "Where are your manners?"

"But she can't hear me."

"She might be able to if she read tealeaves," chuckled Ernie, "You never know when people are into that sort of stuff."

"She was a bit fay," agreed John, "and that's why she grew lavender."

"Lavender," chuckled Freddie, "what's fay about lavender?"

"Ah, you'd be surprised and because I thought it might crop up tonight I looked up the connection before I came out and made a few notes."

"Sounds fascinating, please explain." Dilly leaned back in her chair.

John took a piece of paper from his pocket and unfolded it. "Well, it's said that lavender when used as tea can increase clairvoyance. Something a tealeaf reader like Elizabeth would need, I should imagine."

"Cobblers," said Ernie, "it's just a pretty flower that smells nice."

"It is I agree but listen to this. According to folklore lavender goes back to biblical times and beyond and it's said Cleopatra used its fragrance in her grand seductions. It's even claimed the asp that killed her hid among her lavender bushes. Then there's the religious side of things. Mary, as in mother of Jesus, allegedly draped his clothes on a lavender bush to dry and to transfer his scent to the plant. In fact it was so popular with Christians that they made crosses of lavender to protect themselves from evil." John chuckled, "And then of course there's the magical side. Witches are said to prize lavender for its ability, as I said earlier, to increase clairvoyance. What's more, a mixture of lavender, chamomile, mugwort and rose petals will attract fairies, brownies and elves."

"Brownies," Freddie frowned. "That sounds sinister to me. I mean, why would a witch want to attract young girl guides?"

"Probably not the girl guides," chuckled Ernie, "More likely the American chocolate cakes or cookies as they call them."

John tutted. "It was neither, you Muppets. In this sense a brownie is a good-natured elf that pops along and performs helpful services at night."

"Why at night?" Amelia was confused.

"I've no idea."

"On a more practical note," said Dilly, "lavender's also used for meditation and aromatherapy. I know that because the English teacher in the school where I worked idolised the fragrance because of its calming effect. In fact she always gave us lavender bags at Christmas that she'd made, and bars of soap too."

"Now that's more like it," agreed Amelia, "but I'm afraid the rest is poppycock."

"How about we get back to a more down-to-earth topic," said Freddie, "because I should like to hear what John can tell us about our two houses."

"Yes, that's a good idea," agreed Ernie, "Come on John, let's have some chap's stuff."

Dilly and Amelia both scowled but refrained from commenting.

John returned the lavender folklore notes to his pocket. "Well there were six houses here to begin with and they were known as the Square. Bert's grandfather, George Bray bought them at the beginning of the last century and knocked the two where we are now into one for himself, his wife and family, and at the same time he demolished the ones on either end to make space for parking, storing building materials and so forth. The other two remaining, he saved so that his children would have somewhere to live, should they marry. Sadly that wasn't to be. His son Eric was killed during the Second World War and as I just said Joan left home after a family row. The only one who stayed was Frank who after marrying Ethel moved into half of what is currently your home," he nodded towards Ernie and Amelia, "and then of course on the demise of old George, Frank, his wife Ethel, and young Bert moved in here."

"So what happened to the two houses which are now our Yew Tree Cottage?" Ernie asked, "I mean, who lived in them after Frank, Ethel and Bert moved in here?"

"Frank put in tenants who as you can imagine changed several times over the years. The last were Cyril and Carol Thomas. They lived in the end bit of your place and after the death of his parents, Bert sold it to them along with the one next door which had been empty for years. Cyril and Carol then had the two knocked into one. Of course when he was alive, Frank hoped that the houses would always belong to a Bray, but Bert thought that notion was impractical. With no future generation of Brays on the horizon and him having no desire to have a family, it made sense for him to go against his father's wishes and sell to Cyril and Carol."

"Well, I'm glad he did," said Amelia, "because we love our house."

"Are Cyril and Carol Thomas any relation to Emma Thomas who runs the post office?" Ernie asked.

"Parents," said John. "A year or so after they'd done up your place, Cyril and Carol sold up and bought the post office and general stores. They ran it until they retired and then passed it on to Emma who runs it now with her partner, Steve who also does plumbing."

"Fascinating," said Ernie, "So are Cyril and Carol still around?"

"Cyril is. He lives in one of the bungalows on the Buttercup Field Estate and must be in his eighties now. Carol died a few years back."

"I must try and get to know him then as he'd be able to describe what our place was like before the conversion."

"Why buttercup field?" asked Amelia.

"Would you believe because buttercups grew there? In fact they still do on the rough bits. They were going to give it a Cornish name but as everyone knew the place as the buttercup field, the developers left it as it was."

"One more question," said Freddie, "And then I need to reflect on what we've learned so far. The question being – Frank would have been twenty-seven when war broke out so how did he avoid conscription?"

"Polio," said John, "He had it when a young lad and it left him with a limp. I think that's why everyone had great admiration for him. He worked hard all his life and no-one ever heard him utter any words of self-pity. I know my parents were in awe of him."

"I've one more question too," said Dilly, "then like Freddie I want digest all we've heard. My question being, what can you tell us about the hit and run?"

"Not a lot. It was a subject Bert would never discuss and so we know very little. Having said that, Bert wouldn't have known any more than the rest of us. He was out the night it happened at band practice and got back to find blue lights flashing along the street. He then heard that his dad was dead. Apparently, Frank was on his way home from the pub, inebriated according to the then landlord. It was dark and no-one saw what happened. No-one heard anything either. It was a bloke out walking his dog that found him. He was lying on the side of the road outside the houses in Chapel Terrace, his head in a pool of blood. His leg was broken so it's reckoned he was hit by a passing vehicle, fell backwards and smashed his head on the kerb. The inquest said the blow he received would most likely have caused instant death. Of course the police tried to find out who was driving the car but it was a near impossible task because they reckoned by the nature of the impact there would have been little or no damage to the vehicle involved."

"Oh dear. How awful," tutted Dilly, "Poor Frank, I do wish I'd known him. In fact I'd love to go back in time and see villagers as they were."

"Ah, well I can help you there," said John, "Please don't think I'm being pushy, but from time to time I give a little slide show and lecture on local history and I've one coming up at the pub in November. It'll be a very light-hearted affair and goes down well with the locals. Gail and Robert appreciate it too as it brings in a bit of trade in what is usually a pretty quiet month."

"Excellent," said Dilly. "We'll definitely be there for that. What date is it?"

"We've not settled on a date yet but it'll be in the middle of the month somewhere and most likely on a Wednesday night."

Chapter Six

The weekend weather was dull; the persistent light drizzle caused puddles to form on the uneven path leading to the front door of Lavender Cottage and the gentle south-westerly breeze was too weak to blow along the heavy grey clouds. To make good use of their time indoors, Dilly and Freddie, having agreed Bert's possessions should be gone through, set to emptying cupboards and drawers. Both had already removed his and his parents' clothing from their respective wardrobes and placed all items in a pile on the floor of the spare bedroom.

"I really don't know what to do with this stuff," said Dilly, adding the coats from the pegs in the downstairs hallway to the pile, "Some of it is not good enough for the charity shop but it seems immoral to put any of it out for the dustmen."

"Perhaps we could box it up and store it in the attic. You know. Out of sight out of mind." Freddie pointed to the small ceiling hatch above his head.

"I don't know. Judging by these sloping walls I shouldn't imagine there will be much room up there and there will certainly be no head room. What's more I should imagine it's full of cobwebs, dead creepy crawlies and goodness knows what else."

"I suppose you're right and there's only one way to find out. So I'll take a peep for curiosity's sake if nothing else." Before Dilly could protest, Freddie went downstairs to get his stepladder and torch from the front room.

He only needed to climb two steps in order to reach the hatch which, bearing in mind his godmother's words, he pushed against with caution. A sprinkling of dust fell onto the stepladder as he removed the unhinged door and passed it down to Dilly. After placing it on the floor she passed up the torch.

"Yes, you're right, there's not enough room up here to swing a cat and it's really mucky too. It wouldn't be safe to store anything either as it'd probably bring the ceilings down. Come and have a look." Freddie stepped down from the ladder and passed the torch to Dilly who cautiously climbed a few steps.

"Now that's interesting because it looks to me as though this place might have been thatched once upon a time. There are clumps of long decayed straw or whatever all over the place, but then Denzil did mention that this was one of the oldest houses in the village."

"But surely if it had been thatched it'd have been listed and the thatch would have to stay."

"Not if the roof was replaced before listings became popular. In my opinion lots of places were demolished in the sixties that should have been preserved for posterity." Dilly stepped off the ladder, "Anyway, storing stuff up there is a no-no, so we'll need to come up with another plan." She stepped aside for Freddie to reinstate the hatch, "and I think for now we just leave the clothes here, shut the door and look through some other stuff. You never know we might find something useful. Something that tells us of the Bray family's past."

"I'm with you there." With the hatch back in place, Freddie picked up the step ladder and carried it downstairs. Dilly followed with the torch.

"How about going through the stuff behind the curtain?" said Freddie as he leaned the step ladder against the wall, "I thought it all looked rather interesting when I took out the old tin bath and there are several boxes in there tied up with string."

"The curtain it is then," Dilly pulled aside the thick, brown, heavy fabric and pushed it along the rail as far as it would go. "Where shall we start?"

"Let's start at opposite ends and meet in the middle."

"Good idea," Dilly took two cushions from a bed settee and tossed one to Freddie. "We might as well be comfortable." With enthusiasm tinged with anticipation they both sat down on the floor and began to rummage through the collection of articles.

"I reckon some of this stuff has been here since George Bray bought the houses at the beginning of the last century," said Freddie, opening an old brown suitcase, "Oh, my goodness, yes it has. Look at this." He lifted out an old flat iron and a stone hot water bottle.

"Lovely. When we get straight we'll put them on display somewhere. It'll be nice to have a few bits of history about the place."

The box Dilly was looking through contained tablecloths and curtains. Considering they might come in useful at some point she put them to one side. The next box contained magazines from the nineteen-twenties. "Looks like the Brays were hoarders," she chuckled, "Mind you I'm glad they were because I shall enjoy looking through these magazines on a winter's day." She laughed, "There's a very nice house here for two hundred and ten pounds. I might be tempted to buy it."

"I wonder what people back then would have said if someone had predicted the price of houses today," Freddie closed the suitcase containing the ancient household appliances and reached for a box in the corner.

"They'd have laughed," said Dilly, "thinking they were having their legs pulled."

Because the box Freddie had picked up was quite heavy his hopes were raised as to it containing something of interest and he was not disappointed. "Ah, now this is more like it. Photograph albums."

"Really?" Dilly tossed the magazine she held in her hand back in its box, crawled over to Freddie and looked over his shoulder as he opened up the album. On the first of the yellowing pages was a black and white photograph dated 1930. Set in a studio it was of three young people. Beneath it someone had written, Frank age 18, Eric age 16 and Joan age 12. On the next page in the same setting was a picture of their parents, George and Elizabeth Bray.

"They were a good looking family," said Dilly, "although we already knew that was the case because of the picture of Bert and Frank on the sideboard and Elizabeth above the TV."

The rest of the album contained similar pictures along with a few landscapes, pictures of fishing boats and pictures of gardens. Freddie closed the book and took out another. The first picture was of Eric in uniform dated 1940. Dilly's heart sank. "Such a lovely young man. So tragic that he and so many others lost their lives in such a senseless way."

"I agree," but Freddie not wanting the mood to become maudlin quickly turned the page over. To his surprise the next page was blank except for the words Joan, Easter 1938. There was no picture, just a rectangular white patch where the picture would have been.

"Oh dear," tutted Dilly, "It looks as though Joan's clearing off caused a lot more heartache than I'd imagined."

"More like anger," said Freddie, "They clearly wanted nothing more to do with her. Not that they had any choice because according to John she went off somewhere and was never heard from again."

"Very sad. I wonder what became of her."

"I suppose we could look and see if she's on social media although if she married she'll no longer be a Bray of course."

"I admire your optimism, Freddie, but you're forgetting her age. She was born in 1919 and so would be over a hundred now."

"Damn. In that case there's nothing really we can do."

The next album Freddie pulled from the box was from the nineteen-seventies and the photographs were all in colour. Amongst pictures of the village, the garden, the house, Ethel and Frank, and Bert on his Harley Davidson, was a photograph labelled Cyril and Carol. The striking couple, dressed in beachwear, who were then in their thirties, were sitting on a blanket, eating ice cream.

"That's obviously taken just over the road on the beach," said Dilly, "Look, you can see the roof tops of these houses quite clearly. I recognise the chimney pots."

"Hmm," Freddie was deep in thought.

"A penny for them?" said Dilly.

"Well, I was just thinking that maybe we ought to look this Cyril up while he's still alive. I mean having lived next door to the Brays, he might be able to tell us something useful."

"Well, it wouldn't be much good looking him up if he were not alive but I know what you mean and I agree. If you remember Ernie expressed the desire to meet him too as he should be able to tell him a bit about the layout of his house before it was renovated."

"In which case we'll have a word with Ernie and when he goes to visit Cyril perhaps one of us could go with him."

Dilly stood up. "There's no time like the present so I'll pop round and see him now."

While she was away, Freddie went through a few more boxes. One contained children's toys, mostly vehicles, and judging by the makes and models he estimated they'd be post-war and had most likely belonged to a young Bert. Freddie put them to one side to go through at a later date. In another box he found the trumpet he assumed Bert would have played when a member of the village's brass band. Freddie raised the instrument to his lips and attempted to play it but having no knowledge of embouchure was unable to get out even one note.

On Monday morning, Ernie called in at the village shop to ask Cyril's daughter, Emma if she thought it'd be alright for her father to receive two or three visitors and he explained why. Emma said she could see no reason why not as her father was always ready for a chat but so he would be prepared she rang him to ask. He said he'd be delighted to have visitors and so it was arranged that Ernie, Amelia and Dilly would call on him that afternoon. Freddie would not be able to join them as it was his first day working on the barn conversion at Hilltop Farm.

Chapter Seven

Freddie arrived at the farm just before eight. Aware that he was new to the area, Denzil had given him a detailed description of how to get there thus enabling him to find it with ease.

As the name implied the farm house and buildings were perched on the top of a hill with panoramic views of the sea and surrounding countryside. Denzil's truck was parked alongside a large, granite-built barn surrounded by scaffolding and so assuming it was the barn where he'd be working, Freddie parked there too. Inside he found Denzil drinking tea and talking with three other men. In turn they were introduced and when mugs were empty all began their respective duties. At half past twelve the other men stopped for lunch but as Freddie was dealing with wet plaster he carried on until the wall was as smooth as silk. By then the others had returned to their chores and so Freddie went outside and sat alone on an upturned crate to eat his sandwiches and a thick wedge of cherry cake Dilly had made for a first day treat. Once the food was eaten, he took a short walk along a track towards a field where an aged donkey nodded his head over a sturdy wooden fence. Confident the beast was friendly, Freddie reached out and stroked the donkey's coat. "Hello, mate. How are you doing? I must say you're a fine looking chap."

"His name is Nicholas." Freddie turned as a woman of a similar age to himself approached with a bag of carrots. She wore jeans and a striped shirt and from beneath a floral scarf part-covering her head, wisps of auburn hair framed her attractive face. He smiled. "Nicholas. As in Nicholas Nye?"

"Yes. I take it you're familiar with de la Mare's poem." She seemed pleased with his response and stopped by his side.

"My mother used to read it to me when I was young and for that reason I've always had a soft spot for donkeys."

"Me too." She noted the splashes of plaster on his clothing. "Would I be right in assuming you're the plasterer Denzil was telling me about?" She took a carrot from the bag and held it out to Nicholas.

"I would indeed and my name's Freddie. Freddie Hewitt." He wondered who she was and came to the conclusion she must be the farmer's wife or perhaps even his daughter.

"Excellent," she held out her hand, "delighted to meet you, Freddie. I'm Max."

"Max. Oh. But…but I assumed…I mean, I thought…" He shook her hand hoping he didn't sound as daft as he felt.

"You expected me to be a man." She laughed. "You're not the first to be confused. My name is Maxine. Maxine Eloise Pascoe to be precise. And I should imagine if it was Denzil who told you my name he would purposely have given the impression I was a bloke so you'd be in for a shock. He's like that is Denzil, always up for a joke."

"Hmm, is that so?" Freddie released her hand. "So you run this glorious place? Must be a lot of hard work."

"Yes, it is but I love it." Seeing Nicholas was eating, two horses at the far end of the field crossed for their share.

"Surely you don't run it on your own."

"Goodness me, no. I have two very good and reliable young men who work here full time and I hire seasonal workers when crops need harvesting. I also have my mother but she's in her seventies now and not able to do as much as she once did, due to arthritis. For that reason, just before he died a few years back, Dad put the farm in my name. So now Mum runs the house and looks after the garden and chickens, and I run the farm."

"I see. I hope you don't mind me asking but what are your plans for the barn once its conversion is finished?"

"Of course I don't mind. Most people know anyway. We're diversifying and it's going to be holiday accommodation. Income from farming is greatly affected by the weather and so we decided to opt for a holiday let to give us a bit of security. As you can imagine, Trenwalloe Sands is very popular with tourists." As the horses arrived and nuzzled up to her she fed them both carrots and stroked their manes in turn.

Freddie cast his eyes down the hill and into the valley where beyond the rooftops in the village the sea twinkled in the beams of light from the late September sunshine. "Yes, I can see that a holiday here would be very popular. I mean, with the sea and the countryside people will have the best of both worlds."

"They will. Anyway, would I be right in thinking you're living in Bert Bray's old place?"

"Yes. It belongs to my godmother and I helped her move in. A few days after I got back to the flat I rented she sent me a letter saying there was a room for me at Lavender Cottage should I like the idea. I jumped at the chance and well, here I am."

"Good for you. So you'll be able to help her do the place up."

"Yes, and I look forward to it because at the moment it's like living in the middle of the last century. I love it though and I know it sounds daft but I'm getting used to a primitive way of life. The house has great character too and the fact that Bert's things are still there makes it even more interesting."

Max slowly folded up the bag that had contained carrots and pushed it into the pocket of her jeans. "When you say all Bert's things are still there, what do you mean? I mean, what sort of things?"

"Everything. Clothes, not only his but those of his parents too. Then there are framed photos, photo albums, furniture, pots and pans, crockery, electrical appliances and knickknacks. Everything in fact you'd expect to find in a home."

"Fascinating. Do you think it'd be alright if I came to see the house one day? Before you change things, that is, and I should very much like to have a look at the photograph albums too. I'd like to see a young Bert."

Freddie answered slowly as he tried to fathom out her reason, "Of course, we'd be delighted to show you around."

She smiled sweetly. "I expect you're wondering why I've asked."

"Well, yes. I mean, it does seem a bit odd."

Max looked back at the farmhouse. "Many years ago when my great aunt was a young woman, she and Bert were 'an item'. In fact they were engaged to be married. But for some reason my aunt got cold feet and they had a blazing row. In a fit of anger she threw her engagement ring at him and walked away. When I was young she'd tell me about it. About the guilt she had to live with because she felt she had ruined Bert's life. I mean, don't get me wrong, she was happy for the years she spent with the man she eventually married, but it was the fact Bert never found anyone else that tormented her. He almost became a recluse. He worked hard but apart from playing in the band he seldom socialised despite being gregarious up until the engagement was broken."

"I never knew that. I mean, I knew he'd never married but not the reason why."

"Very few people remember now. It was a long time ago. Well before the swinging sixties."

"I assume then that your great aunt lived here at the farm."

"Until she married Edward, yes. Then she moved to Truro; her husband was a school teacher and taught there."

"I'm not sure why I ask but what was her name?"

"Mary. Mary Lucy Pascoe, and when she married she became Mary Lucy Trelawney."

Chapter Eight

Around the same time that Freddie was chatting to Max at the farm, Dilly, Amelia and Ernie were preparing to visit Cyril Thomas at Daisy Bank, his bungalow on the Buttercup Field Estate over at the far side of the village. And because the afternoon was fine and there was very little wind they agreed to walk not only for the benefit of exercise but to breathe in the fresh sea air also.

"I've popped the nineteen seventies photo album in my bag," said Dilly, as they met outside on the pavement, "I thought Cyril might be able to tell us who some of the people are."

"And I've written out a list of questions," said Amelia, patting the pocket of her jacket, "So I hope he's in a lucid frame of mind."

"I don't think lucidity will be a problem with Cyril. I got the impression from John Martin that he's pretty sharp for his age." Ernie took a packet of humbugs from his pocket and offered it to the ladies.

"Thank you, Ernie," Dilly eagerly took a sweet and unwrapped it, "and I do hope you're right."

Cyril Thomas was sitting by the window in his living room looking out for them. As he saw them turn the corner he left his favourite chair and went into the hallway to open the door and greet them. "Welcome," he said, clearly delighted to have visitors. "Would you all like a cup of tea? I usually have one after my lunch but didn't today as I wanted to wait and have one with you. I've ginger cake too. I popped down to the shop and bought it this morning after Em rang to say you'd be round to see me."

"Sounds lovely," said Amelia, and the others agreed.

"Would you like us to help you make it?" Dilly noted his hands were a little shaky.

"Yes, please. I'm pretty fit and have my marbles but I'm not very good when it comes to carrying things that spill."

When tea was made and the cake was sliced they all went into Cyril's living room where the visitors sat together on the sofa and Cyril returned to his favourite chair by the window.

"Now, Emma tells me you're interested in knowing the layout of the two houses before we had them knocked into one."

Ernie's face lit up. "That's right. If you can remember we'd love to know."

"Or maybe you could draw a little plan for us," suggested Amelia.

"I can do better than that," Cyril left his chair, walked over to the sideboard, took a file from the top drawer and handed it to Ernie. "The architect's plans. They show the original layout of the two houses and where the changes were to be made." Cyril sat down.

Ernie, overwhelmed opened up the file. "But this is wonderful. Would you mind if I borrowed it for a few days so that I can study it in detail?"

"You can keep it. It's no use to me now and Emma hardly remembers the place anyway. It was all a long time ago."

"What can I say then but thank you so much. This really has made my day."

"Do you remember much about the Brays? I mean you must have known them all. Well, Bert and his parents anyway." Dilly glanced at the Brays' nineteen seventies photograph album poking from her bag and found it hard to believe the elderly gentleman opposite was the same young man who sat on the beach with his wife.

"Oh, I remember them all right. Ethel was a smashing woman and a hard worker too. She longed to have the kitchen modernised and a bathroom built. Frank always said he'd do it one day but of course he never did. As far as I know he never even got as far as having plans drawn up. He and Bert were always far too busy to work on their own place."

Dilly smiled. "I remember years ago reading in one of my Anne books someone quoting 'Shoemakers' wives go barefoot and doctors' wives die young'. I suppose the same goes for builders' wives if they're wanting work done to the family home."

"Lucy Maud Montgomery," said Amelia, "Anne's House of Dreams. I've kept all my Anne books and still read them from time to time."

"Really! If you liked the Anne books that really does make us kindred spirits," chuckled Dilly.

Ernie closed the file and placed it on the floor by his feet. "Did you know Bert's grandparents, Cyril? George and Elizabeth I think they were called. They're the folks who bought the houses in the first place."

Cyril shook his head. "No, but I know of them. Elizabeth died when I was a babe in arms and George died a few years later. My mum used to talk about Elizabeth though. She read tealeaves you see and so was very popular with the ladies but I don't think she was very good. She told Mum she'd have a son, so that bit was right, but apparently I was going to be the Chancellor of the Exchequer. Mind you, I got to be a postmaster and did handle money. So perhaps she just got her tealeaves crossed."

"What about the next generation? What was Frank like?" Amelia asked, "We knew Bert of course, but Frank and Ethel had been dead thirty years or more when we moved into Yew Tree Cottage."

"He was alright. Cantankerous at times but then aren't we all? A year or so after we moved to the Square, as it was called then, I asked him if he'd sell us our place and the empty one next door so we could knock 'em both into one but he said no because he wanted to keep all the houses in the family. Not sure why because other than Bert there was no family. His only sister cleared off just before the War and they'd no idea where she went. And as for his brother, the poor soul was killed in action. Looking back I reckon Frank was a bit odd because he seldom mentioned family members and we certainly didn't ask any questions."

"A bit like Bert then," said Amelia, "He never talked of the past."

Cyril laughed. "You're right there. The only subjects that got Bert chatting when he were young were work, the band and his motorbike."

"Have you heard that his old bike turned up the other day?" Dilly chuckled, "We found it bricked up in the pantry of all places."

"Bricked up in the pantry! Why on earth did he do that?"

Having finished her tea, Amelia placed her empty mug on the tray. "That's what we'd like to know."

"Well I knew it'd gone but assumed he'd sold it. He stopped riding it after his parents died, you see. Carol said he probably got rid of it because his mother never liked it but I thought that was daft reasoning."

"Oh well, I suppose we'll never know why he did it," said Dilly, "just as we're unlikely to ever find out what happened to Frank's sister."

"I've just realised that she must have got married because she had a son. Well no, she didn't have to be married, did she? I'm just putting two and two together."

Dilly frowned. "She had a son! How do you know that?"

"Because I saw him. Only briefly, mind you. He turned up at your place late one afternoon back in 1975. He told Frank and Ethel who he was and said his mother was dead and he thought it unfair that she'd got nothing when her father old George Bray died. He left everything to Frank, you see. Frank apparently was furious and said, how could his dad have left her anything when she'd cleared off and no-one knew where she was? Being kind hearted, Ethel suggested they took him on in the business and let him live in the vacant house next door to Carol and me, but the lad was having none of it and said he wanted cash. Frank told him to clear off and then went to the pub in a huff. It was Bert who told me this. You see after his dad had gone to the pub, Bert went outside to clean his motor bike. He always did that when he was upset. Meanwhile the chap who'd be Bert's cousin I suppose, was inside the house where Ethel was giving him something to eat. It was when he came out the back door that I saw him and when it was obvious he wanted to talk to Bert, I made myself scarce and went indoors to tell Carol what I'd heard."

"So Bert did have family," said Dilly.

"Yes, I suppose he did. I never really thought of it like that. Mind you he might not have been genuine. I mean anyone could turn up and say they were Joan's son and no-one would be able to dispute it."

"Any idea what his name was?" Ernie asked.

"I think it was Anthony but I've no idea of his surname. Having said that if his mother never married I suppose it'd be Bray."

"So what happened after this Anthony who claimed to be Joan's son went out to talk to Bert?" Amelia asked.

"I don't know exactly but it was when Frank was coming home from the pub later that night that he was knocked down in the hit 'n run and killed. That's how I know it was in 1975 that the lad turned up."

Dilly gasped. "Might the hit and run driver have been Anthony then?"

Cyril smiled. "Not unless he asked the bus driver who brought him to the village if he could borrow the bus."

"I see. So do you know the exact sequence of events that night?"

"Not really. I know Bert went out around sevenish for band practice and Ethel being upset by the events earlier went to bed around eight with a headache. I was on my own watching the telly because Carol had gone out for a meal with some of her workmates. As for the cousin, I assume he caught a bus out the village after Bert went out. Whatever, he was never seen or heard of again although I think the police tried to find him but not knowing his full name or where he lived they had nothing much to go on and as I said he didn't have a vehicle anyway so couldn't have been involved in the hit and run."

They stayed for another hour. Dilly showed him the photograph album and he was able to identify a few village folks. Amelia also asked the questions listed on her sheet of paper that had not already been covered. To her delight, Cyril was able to answer every one.

Chapter Nine

The following day, Amelia called at Lavender Cottage where Dilly was putting away the vacuum cleaner having just cleaned the highly patterned square carpet hiding a large part of the linoleum covered floor. Ernie was in the back garden tidying up his vegetable plot ready for winter and Freddie was at the farm working on the barn conversion. Glad to have each other to chat with, the two ladies sat down by the Truburn drinking coffee and discussing information gleaned from Cyril the previous day.

"Ernie and I studied the architect's plans for our place last night and they're really fascinating. We've always said we'd love to see how it was in days gone by and the plans are the next best thing."

"I'd like to see how this place was before the two were knocked into one," said Dilly, "but we've not come across anything so I assume any plans were chucked out years ago, which seems a bit odd with the Brays being hoarders."

"Probably never had any plans back then. I mean it must be getting on for a hundred years since this place was done."

"Maybe a bit more. Remember John Martin said Bert's granddad bought the six houses at the beginning of the last century so it could have been as early as 1900 that the end ones were demolished for storage, parking or whatever and these two were knocked into one."

Amelia nodded. "Yes, and it's just occurred to me that any vehicles back then at the turn of the century would have been carts as it'd have been well before motor cars and suchlike were commonplace."

"Of course. I never thought of that. If they had a cart though they must have had a horse unless it was a hand cart."

Amelia cast a glance at the picture of Bert and Frank. "Have you had any more thoughts about Frank's non-accidental accident? Ernie and I chewed over the facts last night but we're none the wiser. And this Anthony chap turning up claiming to be Joan's son seems most peculiar."

Dilly chuckled. "It's all Freddie and I talked about last night. We came up with all sorts of daft ideas and theories but I doubt any of them were near the truth. What really baffled us though was why no-one had ever mentioned Anthony before. Anyway, we've decided not to make a big thing of it but we're planning to go to the pub tonight and if John Martin is in we'll ask him what he knows. I mean he must have heard about Joan's boy turning up."

Amelia placed her empty coffee mug on the arm of her chair. "Probably forgotten though. It seems it was only a flying visit and if John didn't actually see him it wouldn't have imprinted itself on his brain."

"True. Anyway, do you and Ernie fancy joining us for a drink tonight?"

"That'd be lovely and I don't need to ask Ernie because he likes to pop to the pub during the week because it's quieter than the weekend and so easier to chat with his mates."

They all met up at seven-thirty and then made their way through the village to the Duck and Parrot. Half way along the long stretch of road, Dilly slowed and pointed to a row of houses opposite. "Is that Chapel Terrace? I ask because it's next to a chapel."

"Correct," said Amelia, "but the chapel is no longer used for services and closed shortly before we moved here. I believe it now belongs to the owner of the petrol garage."

"In that case it must be somewhere over there that Frank was knocked down," said Freddie.

"Yes, I suppose so. I must admit I've never thought of that before. Mind you, until the other day when John mentioned where it'd happened, we'd not known the exact spot, had we, Ernie?"

"No, we just knew it was along the main road somewhere."

The bar was fairly quiet as they stepped inside the pub, but through the open door of the adjoining games room, drifted tinkles of happy laughter and lively female chatter.

"Sounds like the ladies darts' team are having a practice," said Ernie, as they seated themselves around a table by the window and Freddie went to the bar for drinks.

"Darts. I wouldn't mind having a go at that," said Dilly, "I haven't played for a while but I was always quite good."

"You must give them a nod then," said Ernie, "because they're always on the lookout for new talent."

"Who's the team leader, captain or whatever they're called then?" asked Amelia.

"Dotty Gibson," Ernie removed his jacket and hung it on the back of his chair.

Dilly raised her eyebrows. "You mean the jogger blogger?"

Ernie nodded. "Yep."

"Well, I'll go for that then because she's already said if I'd like to I'd be welcome to go jogging with her, so if I get the chance to have a chat I'll be able to kill two birds with one stone."

Amelia thinking she must have misheard, frowned. "Did I hear right? You're into jogging? I mean, is it safe at your age?"

"Yes and why not. Obviously I wouldn't attempt a marathon without the necessary training but I'll have no problem jogging round the village. At my own pace of course."

Ernie chuckled. "That's what comes of being a gym mistress, I suppose. Having said that it must be a few years since you retired now."

"Coming up for ten but let's not get on the subject of time."

Freddie arrived with the drinks on a tray. "John's in. He's sitting over in the corner near the fireplace with a chap wearing a dog collar. So unless he's off to a fancy dress party I assume the bloke in question is the vicar."

"Yes, that'll be the Reverend Peter Goodman. He and John get on very well." Ernie took his pint of beer from the tray, "Cheers Freddie."

"Yes cheers," Amelia raised her glass too.

"Well we don't want to interrupt John while he's talking to the vicar," said Dilly, as Freddie returned the tray to the bar, "So we'll have to be patient."

"Vicar won't be here much longer," said Ernie, "He usually pops in for half a bitter and then goes home. I've never known him stay later than half eight although if there's something special on, like a charity do, he'll stay a bit longer then."

Just before half eight they saw the vicar rise and heard him say goodnight to John and then to the licensees as he passed the bar on his way to the back door.

Freddie picked up his glass of lager. "I'll go and have a quick word with John now in case he wants to get off home too."

Freddie was away for a little more than ten minutes.

"Any luck?" Dilly asked.

"Yes and no." He sat back down. "John was surprised to hear about Joan's son but said he was away on holiday when Frank was killed and so he supposes that tragedy would have overshadowed Anthony's brief visit, meaning he never got to hear of it."

"And I daresay very few people knew he'd been here anyway because as far as we know only Frank, Ethel and Bert saw him." Ernie drained his glass and stood, "Anyway, my round. Same again for everyone?" All nodded.

Dilly handed Ernie her empty glass. "And Cyril," she said. "He saw him briefly and told Carol about him."

"Yes, you're right. I'd forgotten Cyril." Ernie stacked the empty glasses and carried them to the bar.

Amelia addressed Freddie. "John not knowing of Anthony's visit is obviously the *no* bit of your comment but what's the *yes* bit?"

Freddie waved as John walked towards the door zipping up his fleece top. "He's going to try and find out on-line by looking on the family history website he's a member of. It won't be easy though because we've no idea whereabouts in the country she went. It's marriages he'll be looking at from 1939 onwards. 1939 being the year Joan left home in a huff. He's hoping the fact her middle name was Jago might make her stand out."

"Jago! Why on earth did her parents give her that for a middle name?" Amelia was nonplussed.

"Must be because it was her mother's maiden name," said Dilly, "According to the marriage certificate we found, her mother was Elizabeth Jago before she married George Bray."

"Makes sense, I suppose, but I'm surprised John knows that."

"Well if you remember he told us his mum and Joan were friends and the same age," Freddie reminded her, "so I expect he remembers his mum saying. I mean, her full name would have been on the school register."

As Ernie returned with the drinks and sat down, the ladies having finished their darts practice entered the bar from the games room. Leading the way was Dotty chatting to Max.

Max's face lit up when she saw Freddie. "Hi, lovely to see you again."

"And you too."

"And would this be your godmother?" Max smiled at Dilly.

"Yes, and these good people are our neighbours, Ernie and Amelia Trewella, but then you probably already know that."

"I do, yes. Ernie's often here when we're practising and gives us a bit of moral support when we have home matches."

"Well, if you'd like another team member I'd love to join you," said Dilly, "I know I'm not in the first flush of youth but I've a good eye and a steady hand."

"We're none of us in the first flush of youth," laughed Max, "and you'd be very welcome."

"Lovely, and while you're here, Dotty, I'd like to take you up on your invitation for a jog."

"Brilliant. I'll pick you up at yours at ten tomorrow morning, if that's okay."

"Sounds fine."

"And we'll be here next Tuesday for a darts practice if you'd like to join us, Dilly," Max winked at Freddie, "and I'll see you tomorrow."

Dotty and Max said goodbye and went off to refill their empty wine glasses.

"Looks like you have a couple of admirers," chuckled Amelia, "and neither of those girls are married.

"Dotty has a boyfriend though," Ernie reminded her, "and he's a copper."

"Yes, of course. Nice lad Gerry."

Dilly heartened by the twinkle in her godson's eyes, placed her hand beneath the table and crossed her fingers.

Chapter Ten

The following day, Freddie arrived home from work just after five. He parked as usual down the side of the house and went in through the back door. "Hmm something smells nice."

"It's a combination of chicken and bacon lasagne and a cinnamon and apple cake. They're in the oven together."

"Lovely. My favourites." Freddie took off his jacket and hung it in the hall.

"Any news from John?" Dilly asked.

Freddie shook his head. "Not yet." He sat down and removed his boots, "How did the jog go?"

"Really well. Dotty is good company and there's no doubt that she's the one to go to for gossip. She knows who lives in every house and gave me a running commentary as we jogged around the village."

"Pity she wasn't here in 1975 when Frank was killed and Anthony turned up but I suppose she wasn't even born then."

"No she wasn't. She was forty earlier this year according to Ernie and Amelia."

"Same age as Max then."

Dilly raised her eyebrows. "Been having a cosy chat with her then?"

Freddie laughed. "Not today, no, and it was Denzil who told me how old she is and that's because she's the same age as him. In fact there's just one day between them and their mothers were in the hospital maternity ward at the same time. For that reason when they were at primary school their parents arranged for them to have joint birthday parties and Denzil was saying what fun they were because if the weather was good they'd party on the beach."

"What a lovely idea."

Freddie was about to reply when his phone rang. It was a number he didn't recognise. "Hello," his face lit up. After a few words, Dilly realised the caller must be John. While they were talking she quietly made two mugs of tea and set one down on the floor beside Freddie's chair.

"Good news?" she eagerly asked as he returned the phone to his pocket.

"Yes, I think we can say that. John apologised for not ringing earlier but his laptop was playing up this morning so he's only just got round to looking Joan up." Freddie picked up his mug of tea, "Anyway, he's found out something about her. In August 1939 she married a Brian Hammond at a registry office in Plymouth. He's down as a farm worker and in January the following year they had a son, Anthony."

"So she must have got married a month or so after she left here because John said the other day that she left early in the summer of 1939."

"And no doubt that was what the family row was about. Her wanting to marry this Brian Hammond, I mean."

"You're right, because at that time she would have only been twenty and so unable to marry without her parents' consent. Coming of age was twenty-one back then."

"That figures, because according to John, who also looked up her birth registry, she was twenty-one a week before the marriage."

"Oh dear," sighed Dilly, "and that's no doubt why they didn't marry straight away after she left even though they wanted to. What's more, a quick calculation tells me she would have been pregnant when the row took place and no doubt that was the reason behind it. How times have changed."

"Yes. Anyway, at least we have a name now. For Anthony Hammond, that is."

Dilly looked at the clock and saw it was time to take the cake from the oven. "I wonder what happened to Anthony. He'd be eighty-two now so probably still around."

"That's what John said. He'd looked for deaths in the Plymouth area but with Anthony Hammond being quite a common name he had no luck. He might not even have lived in Plymouth for long. We know he was born there but that means nothing."

"And I suppose it doesn't really matter anyway." Dilly placed the cake tin on a table-mat and removed her oven gloves. "I can't help but wonder if he was responsible for Frank's death though."

"Well admittedly he certainly had a motive but the fact he didn't have a vehicle makes it highly unlikely."

"Yes, you're right. So really learning Anthony's surname hasn't helped at all."

"No, but it has tied up a loose end. Now we just need to fathom out why Bert bricked up his motorbike and who knocked down Frank."

Dilly returned to the chair she had vacated. "And that reminds me. Amelia popped round this morning to say Ernie was spending the day going through his big shed. I went out later to see how he was getting on and he had a pile of stuff on the back path destined for the recycling centre. He got it done anyway and so now he has room for the motorbike. He's coming round in the morning to pick it up and hopes to have it up and running in a few days. Unless he has to get new parts, that is."

"Brilliant. I look forward to seeing it done and probably even taking it for a spin."

"Me too. Seeing it, that is. Not taking it for a spin. Anyway, while it's gone it'll give me the opportunity to clean out the old pantry. I hate knowing all that muck's in there. All forty-seven years' worth of it."

"So are we going to put the bike back in there when it's done?"

"I suppose we'll have too. At least until we decide what to do with it."

Chapter Eleven

The following morning, after Freddie had gone off to work, Ernie as pre-arranged collected the motorbike and wheeled it slowly to his shed, careful to avoid damaging the flat tyres even though he expected they had perished many years' before and would be useless. No sooner had he gone than Amelia called round for a chat.

"I'm glad you're here," said Dilly, "because I keep meaning to ask if Bert used to dig up his dahlias to over-winter them?"

Amelia sat down. "No. He told me he used to when he first started growing them but then realised as winters down here are usually mild it's not necessary. He used to keep an eye on the weather though and if we were in for a cold spell he'd spread straw over the garden. I only remember him doing it once though and that was in 2018 when we had the Beast from the East. Even then he cursed it because the straw blew around in the wind."

"I'll do the same then and keep my fingers crossed that straw's not necessary."

Amelia chuckled. "Well if you do need some I'm sure Max Pascoe would be only too happy to pass on a couple of bales if you send young Freddie up to the farm."

Dilly was just about to comment on Amelia's words when the back door opened and closed and Ernie rushed into the room. "Sorry to barge in but it's just that, well, I think you'll want to see this." He held up two sheets of discoloured paper with creases where they had been folded.

"You're shaking," Amelia stood up and guided her husband to a vacant armchair.

"What is it, Ernie?" Dilly was alarmed to see her usually calm neighbour clearly anxious.

Ernie took in a deep breath. "Well, it's like this. After I'd put the bike in the shed I took the manual and leather gloves out from under the seat and put them on top of my workmate. Shortly after I needed to look something up and so reached for the manual. When I opened it up, an old photo and these bits of paper fell out. I think you'll find them interesting. In fact, I know you'll find them interesting." He passed the photo and papers to Dilly, took in another deep breath and leaned his head back in the chair.

Not knowing what to expect, Dilly, with shaking hands spread the papers out on her lap. "My goodness. This is dated January 1976."

"Really!" Amelia, glad to see her husband had calmed down looked over Dilly's shoulder, "But that's the year after Frank was killed."

Ernie nodded. "Exactly, and look at the photo."

The picture was of three people on a beach. A man and a woman were sitting on a blanket and a young boy was building a sand castle. There was nothing written on the back other than the date – July 1948.

"Who are they?" Dilly passed the picture to Amelia.

Ernie unzipped his fleece top. Glad his heart rate was back to normal. "Read the note, letter or whatever you want to call it and then you'll see."

"Yes, please do as I'm longing to know what it says." Amelia laid the photo on the arm of her chair and sat back down, her eyes transfixed on the sheets of paper.

Dilly reached for her reading glasses. "Well as you can see it's handwritten but I can't see by whom," she turned the papers over, "My goodness, it's written by Bert. He's signed his name at the bottom of the second sheet. But then I suppose that makes sense since the bike belonged to him." Dilly saw a flicker of impatience in Amelia's eyes, "Sorry, right. Well, here goes."

January 1976.

I've no idea who you are likely to be but whoever, if you have found this letter, then you'll also have found my bike. I've not been gifted with a wonderful imagination but even so I expect you'll be flummoxed as to why some long dead bloke would brick up his bike in the first place. And I am dead, because were I still alive there's no way you or anyone else would get near my pantry. Or should I say, Mum's pantry.

I'm a builder and Bert Bray is my name. I live here at Lavender Cottage, a name given to the house by my lovely grandmother, Elizabeth, who, would you believe, loved lavender. I prefer dahlias myself but that's another story. Originally there were six houses here. All bought by my granddad, George Bray in 1902. The first thing Granddad (who was also a builder) did after the purchase was to demolish the ones on either end and then knock these two into one. The other two are going to get the same treatment from Cyril and Carol Thomas who are in the throes of buying the house they rent and the empty one next to it. I'm sure that by the time whoever you are reading this that the work will have long been done but I've no idea if Cyril and Carol will still be there.

You're probably wondering why I'm waffling and I can't say as I blame you. The reason is though that I'm not quite sure how to say what I need to say as it's about my dad's death. You see, Dad, who was called Frank, was knocked down in a hit and run four months ago and he was killed. And as if that wasn't bad enough, my poor old mum, shocked and heartbroken by his going, suffered a massive heart attack that took her as well.

The day Dad was killed was a funny old day. It was Monday, September 1st and we, that is Dad and me, had finished work early because the job we'd been working on was done and it was too late in the day to start another and so we went to the builders' merchants on the way home, had a natter with the lads there and arrived back here about the same time as usual. No sooner had we got in than there was a knock on the door. Mum answered and led a bloke we'd never seen before into our living room. He said his name was Anthony Hammond and he was my Auntie Joan's son. Auntie Joan being Dad's sister. I remember her but only vaguely because she up and scarpered in 1939 when I'd have been just four years old. Dad was quite hostile and when Anthony said he thought his mother should have had a share of the family's wealth, he went nuts and said how could she have got a share when no-one knew where she was and I must admit I agree with him. To try and keep the peace, Mum suggested Anthony come and work in the family business. She even suggested he live in the empty house next to Cyril and Carol that they are now buying. Obviously he said no, otherwise Cyril and Carol wouldn't be buying it, would they? Anyway, the hostility continued and it was horrible. In the end, Dad, red in the face and swearing like a trooper, grabbed his jacket and his baccy tin and said he was going to the pub and he expected Anthony gone when he got back. We all breathed a sigh of relief when we heard the front door slam and Mum being Mum offered Anthony a cup of tea and a bite to eat which he willingly accepted. As for myself, I was shaking like a leaf and so went out the back and started to clean my bike. While I was there Cyril came out of his house and I told him what'd happened. Half an hour or so later, our back door opened and out came Anthony, and Cyril being diplomatic went back into his place. Thankfully I'd calmed down by then and so Anthony and me chatted in a friendly manner *and I must admit I liked him and part of me felt sorry for him. He told me a bit about his mum, my Auntie Joan, and how she'd led him to believe she had no family living. He knew she came from Cornwall but had no idea where and he never asked. His dad, who was called Brian, worked on a farm in the Plymouth area and lived in a tied cottage. It was when he came to Cornwall for a holiday at Easter in 1939 that Joan and Brian met. Anthony said his mum claimed it was love at first sight and they wrote to each other every day for a month after he went home until Joan decided to leave her job and everything behind to be with him. They married soon after but when Anthony was eight and a half years old his dad was killed in an accident on the farm and so to make sure they could stay in the cottage his mother took over the work his father had done. A few years later, the farmer said that she could stay in the cottage for as long as she wanted whether she continued working on the farm or not.*

Anthony left home when he was eighteen and joined the Navy where he served for twelve years. When he came out he got a job in Plymouth as a sales assistant in a gents outfitters and then in 1975 his mother had a stroke. It was as she lay dying that she told him she'd lied about having no family and that her father had a building business and owned several houses and in retrospect she felt she should have benefited from the family's modest wealth. After she died, Anthony found our address amongst her possessions along with her birth and marriage certificates. Knowing where we lived he vowed he'd come to Cornwall to find us.

After he'd finished telling me about himself, I wanted to help him. I told him that I wasn't in a position to do anything at that time but promised when it came to me inheriting the houses and business I'd make sure he got a fair share and we vowed to keep in touch. Meanwhile, I gave him the copper bracelet given to me by my grandfather George Bray shortly before he died. Granddad wore it to help relieve the pain of arthritis and his name was engraved on its inside. Anthony was delighted and slipped it on his wrist. After all George was his grandfather just as much as he was mine and I thought it only fair he had something belonging to the granddad he never knew. I then noticed it was time for me to get off to band practice and Anthony said he'd finish cleaning the bike for me. To show there were no hard feelings I told him he could take it for a spin if he wanted before he caught the bus back to the railway station at St Austell. He said he'd love to do that and he'd make sure the bike was back in place and he'd gone before Dad got back from the pub.

I don't know what happened next but at half past nine when I got back from the practice there were flashing blue lights along the main street and two police officers were knocking on our door. Mum didn't hear them because she was in bed and out like a light having taken sleeping pills. The police told me there had been an accident. Someone had knocked Dad down but not stayed to report it. Dad must have been in the road, probably crossing, because apparently he was knocked backwards and had hit his head on the kerb. They believe he died instantly.

It wasn't until the next morning that I remembered Anthony and the bike. I went out to check and saw it wasn't where I'd left it, meaning Anthony must have taken it out. It then occurred to me that he had a very strong motive to see my dad dead. I'd told the police the night before about the visit from my cousin and the bitterness it caused which sent Dad to the pub, but when they heard he'd arrived on the bus I think they dismissed him as being a likely suspect but said they'd try and locate him. I heard no more and suppose they'd had no luck. A few days later Mum died and then a week or so after that Cyril asked if he could buy their house and the empty one next door. I jumped at the chance so that if Anthony did make contact I'd be able to give him the money the sale raised and therefore keep my promise. But I never heard from him and eventually I convinced myself that in a fit of anger he must have mowed Dad down on my bike. Realising then it was a stupid thing to have done, he fled never to return again.

After that I viewed my bike, my once pride and joy, with disdain. Yesterday I cleared out the pantry and wheeled it inside and today I write this rather long-winded epistle which I'll put inside the manual underneath the seat before I brick the pantry up. And so whoever you are I leave the consequences in your hands. Is my cousin guilty and where is he now? If he ran Dad down hoping for money, why hasn't he been in touch? He didn't leave his address so I've no way of contacting him. I do know though that he was born on January 3rd 1940 so I'll leave it to you to work out his age. Apart from that, all I know is what I've told you. By the way, the photo was given to me by Anthony. It's of him, my Auntie Joan and her husband, Brian who I suppose would be my uncle.

Good luck to you if you try and work it out.

Cheers,
Bert Bray.

PS. Should you get the bike up and running her name is Lizzy. I tell you that because she responds to her name and so it might help.

Chapter Twelve

Freddie arrived home from work to find Dilly looking flustered as she busily polished the furniture. She glanced up from the sideboard as he entered the room. "Ah, good you're back. Now if you pop down to Yew Tree for a shower this instance dinner will be ready by the time you get back."

"Okay, but why do you look all hot and bothered?"

"Because I need to get everything straight before half past six. Oh, fiddle, I didn't mean to say that. Now I've let the cat out of the bag."

"You didn't mean to say what?" Freddie placed his empty lunch box on the table and hung the keys to his van on a hook by the fireplace. "And what's on at half past six?"

"Oh dear, I didn't want to tell you until you were relaxed and we're having dinner but I suppose I'll have to now."

"Well, I'm sure whatever you have to say can't be that earth shattering, so if you'd rather leave it a while I'll go and have a shower as you suggested."

"Bless you. Off you go then."

Freddie pointed to the ceiling. "Is it alright if I pop upstairs and get a change of clothes?"

"Yes, yes of course." Dilly disappeared inside the walk-in cupboard beneath the stairs with the furniture polish and duster and re-emerged with the vacuum cleaner, "And don't ask Amelia or Ernie what's on at half past six."

"I won't."

Twenty minutes later, Dilly and Freddie were sitting at the table in the living room to plates of mashed potatoes, sausages and peas.

"Okay, so what's going on? It must be quite something because Amelia and Ernie were both acting as nutty as you."

Dilly looked at the clock. "That's because we're having a meeting at half past six to discuss this." She took the photograph and letter from the pocket of her cardigan and passed both across the table.

Freddie put down his knife and fork, took the offerings and slowly unfolded the sheets of paper. The photograph slipped out. He looked at it and frowned. "What? Who?"

"Read what the letter says."

Dilly watched her godson as he read Bert's letter, his face changing from a frown to one of wonder. When he reached the end he placed the papers on the table and picked up his knife and fork. "My mind's in a whirl. I really don't know what to say."

"Exactly," said Dilly, "and that's why we're having a meeting," she looked at the clock, "in forty-two minutes."

"We being Amelia, Ernie and the two of us I assume."

"And John so that he can get onto his family history site because we need to track this Anthony down."

"Ideal."

"And then there's Dotty."

Freddie looked up from his plate. "Dotty!"

"Yes, she's coming too."

"But why?"

"Because after Ernie, Amelia and I had briefly discussed the letter we went our separate ways to think over what we'd read. Ernie returned to doing up the bike, Amelia set to tidying up the cupboard under their sink and me, I went out into the front garden to cut back the dying foliage on the dahlias ready for winter."

"And?"

"Oh, yes, and while I was out there Dotty came jogging along the road. When she saw me she stopped and asked if I wanted to join her but I said not today as I had things on my mind. She looked puzzled so I told her about the letter and photo. She was fascinated. I said we were having a meeting tonight to see if we could get to the bottom of it and she begged me to let her come too because Gerry was on the night shift and so she'd be all alone. I thought why not. She's nice and might even be able to contribute something. I know she's not been in the village all that long but at least she keeps her ears open."

"Yes, true. She might be able to help and the more the merrier."

"Anyway, we need to eat up, get the washing up done and prepare the room for our guests."

They finished their meal in silence. Freddie then washed up and Dilly dried.

"If there are six of us we ought to pull out the leaves of the table," said Freddie, "then we can sit one on each end and two along each side."

"Excellent idea." They moved the chairs to one side and then each pulled out a leaf.

"Bother," said Dilly, "it looks really odd with Formica on the main part but not the leaves."

"It does but didn't you find some old tablecloths behind the curtain?" Freddie asked.

"Good point. I did so I'll go and see what I can find."

"And I'll come with you because we'll need a couple more dining chairs and there are several in the front room."

The only oblong tablecloth large enough to cover the extended table was a brightly coloured affair with large pink and red roses on a blue and white background. It smelled a bit musty but was a perfect fit.

"My mum had one similar to this when I was young so I reckon it's a relic from the nineteen-fifties." Having put the cloth in place, Dilly smoothed out a few creases with her hand.

"Goes well with the room's ancient décor then," chuckled Freddie, "despite the clashing colours and patterns."

"It does, but then that's how things were backalong. People had to make do and mend because the world wasn't awash with throwaway stuff like it is today." Dilly bent down and took two bottles of wine from the lower cupboard of the kitchen cabinet and placed them on the table, "I hope two bottles will be enough."

"Hmm, had I known about this get-together I'd have grabbed a couple more from the post office on my way home."

"I don't think you would have," said Dilly, "because I'm pretty sure they don't have a license."

"You're right. I could still have gone to the off licence though but it's too late now."

The back door opened. "Coo-ee. Only us. Can we come in?"

"Of course," Dilly opened the door leading into the kitchen to greet them as they climbed the three steps.

"I know we're a bit early but I wanted to see if there's anything we can do to help," said Amelia.

Ernie chuckled. "Don't believe a word of it. She's been hovering by the door for half an hour now wishing the time away."

"Well it is rather exciting, don't you think? I mean, tonight we might be able to solve a crime committed nearly fifty years ago." Amelia noticed the bottles on the table, "Oh, are we having wine?"

Dilly nodded. "Yes, and hopefully we'll have something to celebrate."

"In which case I'll go and grab a couple of bottles of my elderberry," said Ernie, "We don't want to run out."

"I didn't know you made wine," said Dilly.

"I've been doing it since I retired. Be back in a mo."

"His wine is very nice," said Amelia, as Ernie left the house, "but it is inclined to be rather on the strong side. His latest batch is blackberry but he only started it the other day so it won't be ready for at least a year."

As Ernie returned with two bottles of elderberry wine, there was a knock on the front door.

"Come in, come in," Dilly stood aside for John to enter the hall. He carried not only his laptop but a bottle of merlot. Five minutes later, Dotty arrived. With her she had a bottle of chardonnay.

"Great minds think alike," she said as she put her bottle on the table with the others, "It's been in the fridge so it's already chilled."

"Well let's hope our great minds can come up with something positive tonight," said Amelia.

Dilly placed six glasses on the table. "Now we're all here, shall we sit?"

"Anywhere in particular?" Ernie asked.

"No, no. Sit wherever you like." Dilly sat along one side of the table and Amelia sat down beside her. Ernie sat at the end nearest the Truburn and John at the other so that he was near the electricity socket above the cooker. Down the side opposite Dilly and Amelia, Freddie sat and Dotty placed herself beside him.

John plugged in his laptop, opened it up and logged onto his family history site while everyone else filled their glasses with wine and Amelia poured a glass for John.

"Right, I'm ready to go. What's Joan's boy called again?"

"Anthony Hammond and I've just realised you've heard about the letter but not seen it yet, John." Dilly stood up and took it from the sideboard.

"You read it out," said Amelia, "because I should like to hear it again. And as well as John, Dotty's not read it either."

"Okay," Dilly did as suggested and all listened, not wanting to miss any salient points.

"Right, so the obvious place to start is to search for this Anthony Hammond. We already know he was born on January the third 1940 and the name of his parents, so I'll see if I can find him in deaths." John typed the name in the search box. "Damn, as I thought there are dozens."

"But they won't all be the right age surely," said Freddie.

"They will be thereabouts because I gave his year of birth to help the search. Of course it doesn't help us not knowing whether he's dead or alive. I mean, if he's not dead we're not going to find him in deaths, are we?"

"No, and what's more, if he is still around we've no idea where he's living now," said Amelia, "I mean, he'd have retired years ago so could be just about anywhere."

"How about trying Facebook," Dotty suggested, "I know lots of oldies who use it including my gran."

Dilly looked over the top of her reading glasses. "Less of the oldies, young lady."

"Oh, I didn't mean to cause offence. It was meant in a kindly way. My gran's as bright as a button."

"And to be fair we are oldies," chuckled Amelia.

"Okay, try Facebook then, John."

"I'm already on it but having no luck so far."

"He probably calls himself Tony anyway," said Freddie, "most Anthonys do."

"I know," John went back to his family history site, "I'll just type his name in the search box and see if it comes up with a mention of him in a newspaper article or something like that."

After a few minutes searching, John tutted, leaned back in his chair and drained his glass. As he placed it on the table, Amelia refilled it and also her own. Everyone else around the table was already on their second glass hoping the alcohol would stimulate their thoughts.

"Is it worth trying marriages?" said Dilly, "We know he wasn't married in 1975 but he'd only have been thirty-six then so could have married after that."

"Good idea, and if he worked in a gents outfitters in Plymouth the chances are he'd still be there then especially with Joan, his mum being in the area, although according to Bert's letter she'd died by 1975." John tried marriages in Plymouth. There were several for Anthony Hammond in the seventies and eighties but not knowing the name of his likely wife it was impossible to know which path to go down.

"How about looking for him on a census," said Amelia, "I mean, isn't that what genealogists do? We know he lived in Plymouth in 1975 so that way we could get an address."

"It is what genealogists do but unfortunately census returns are only made public after one hundred years, so we'll have to wait until 2071 to see details of the 1971 census."

"Damn. I don't think we can wait that long." Dilly finished her wine and refilled her glass.

Freddie did likewise and topped up Dotty's glass too.

"Before I drink any more I must pop to the bathroom." Dotty stood, pushed back her chair and glanced around the room, "Which way is it please?"

Amelia choked on her wine. Dilly slapped her hand across her mouth. "Oh, dear."

"Is there a problem?" Dotty was confused.

"No problem," chuckled Freddie, "Just no bathroom."

Dotty frowned. "But…"

"We have a very nice loo at the bottom of the garden. Come with me and I'll point it out to you."

Dilly led Dotty down the three steps and into the kitchen.

"Oh my god. Surely you don't cook in here. It's freezing."

"I agree it is freezing and no we don't cook in here. The cooker is in the living room and so is the kitchen cabinet and all our utensils."

"Of course. Silly me. I remember seeing the cooker now before I sat down but I'd forgotten because I had my back to it."

Dilly opened the back door. "We'll bring the place into the twenty-first century one day, Dotty, but for now we have to pretend it's a century earlier." She pointed down the garden path: "the loo is down there where you can see a flickering light over the top of the door from a little paraffin lamp on a ledge."

"Not too far then."

"No, but you'll need this," Dilly took a blue plastic bucket from beneath the sink, filled it with cold water and handed it to Dotty. "When you get back you can wash your hands in the sink here. I'm afraid there's only cold water though."

Dilly returned to the living room and chuckled as she sat down. "That was a sight to behold. Dear Dotty teetering down the garden path in high heels carrying a bucket of water."

"Poor girl," said Amelia, "When I need to go I'll pop home and then leave the door unlocked so that anyone can use our bathroom if they prefer."

"Will Oscar be alright with that?" John asked.

"Yes, he loves people but I'll shut him in the other room just to be on the safe side."

A few minutes later they heard the back door open and then water running from the tap.

"Did you get on alright?" Dilly laughed, as Dotty returned to the room and sat down.

"Yes, thanks but it's really spooky out there with a half moon and twinkling stars. I imagined Brays from backalong tripping down the path and the ladies in long frocks."

"Would they have been in long frocks then?" Freddie asked.

Dilly nodded. "If George bought the houses in 1902, then yes. It was only a year after Queen Victoria died."

"And talking of dying," said Dotty, "I should imagine lots of the Brays died here in this house." She took a sip of wine. "I could almost feel their presence out there with the wind rustling the leaves and the moon peeping in and out of the dark clouds."

Dilly shuddered. "Yes, I suppose they must have. George and Elizabeth anyway. Bert too of course and his mother, Ethel. But not Frank. We know he died out in the street."

"And the houses were here for donkey's years before the Brays bought them anyway," said Freddie, "So loads of unknowns must have popped their clogs here too."

Dotty looked over her shoulder. "It's just a thought," she whispered, "but since it's a spooky old night and we're not getting anywhere with our hunt for Anthony online, why don't we have a séance. That way we can ask Frank who was driving the vehicle that knocked him down. I mean, at the moment we don't know that it was Anthony. It's just old Bert putting down his thoughts."

"Excellent idea," enthused Dilly.

"It is," agreed John, "but there's something we're missing and that's a medium."

"Bother, I didn't think of that," Dotty looked downcast.

Dilly feeling likewise, sighed deeply.

"I know," Amelia gleefully clapped her hands, "Let's use an Ouija board instead."

"Yes, of course," gushed Dilly, "We won't need a medium for that."

"No, but we will need an Ouija board," laughed Ernie, "so unless Dilly has one tucked away somewhere, that's another dead end."

"Dead end," giggled Dotty, as she refilled her glass. "You are a card, Ernie."

"Card, yes of course. Since we don't have an Ouija board we must make one," said Amelia, "Do you have any old bits of card, Dilly?"

Dilly stood up. "Yes, there are all sorts of bits and bobs in the recycling bag." She walked into the cupboard under the stairs and came out with a flattened teabag box, two flattened cereal boxes and the packaging from new bedding she had recently purchased.

"Excellent. Now we need scissors and pens, preferably felt tipped."

Dilly took two pairs of scissors and two pens, one black the other blue, from a drawer in the kitchen cabinet. Amelia then gave instructions and the team set to creating a makeshift Ouija board under her supervision. Dilly and Dotty cut the cardboard into approximately two inch square pieces. On each of twenty-six squares, Freddie wrote one letter of the alphabet. On ten, John wrote out the numbers 0 – 9 and on two, *yes* and *no*. Meanwhile, Ernie refilled the glasses.

John closed the lid of his laptop and placed it on the sideboard. "I hate to be a dismal Jimmy but in my experience homemade Ouija boards are too easy to manipulate."

"You've done this before then?" Freddie was surprised.

"Yes, back when I was young and gullible. It was all the rage then but I must admit it was great entertainment."

"As will be our little venture," Amelia looked up at the solitary light hanging from the middle of the beam, "I think to create the right atmosphere we must switch off the light and have candles instead."

"Now that I don't think we can do," said Dilly, "Unless you've seen some somewhere, Freddie."

He shook his head, "I'm afraid not."

"No worries. We have some at home. Be a sweetheart, Ernie and go and fetch them please. There are definitely some in the cupboard under the sink because I saw them earlier today."

Ernie arrived back with four candles and two more bottles of elderberry wine.

"Well done," Amelia rose to take the candles, "Do you have any old saucers or something to stand them on, Dilly?"

"Bert's jam jars." Dilly hurried out to the pantry, picked up four jars, washed them under the tap and dried them on the hand towel hanging on the back door. While Amelia put the candles in the jars, lit them and placed them around the room, Dilly spread out the handwritten cards in a circle on the table and stood a clean, empty wine glass upside-down in the middle. She clapped her hands. "All ready now."

Amelia sat down. "This is so exciting."

Freddie convinced a cold draught had suddenly come from nowhere wasn't so sure.

"So what do we do now?" Dotty asked.

"We contact a spirit," said Amelia, "and ask it questions."

"So who's going to be question master?" John asked.

"Perhaps, to make it fair we should take it in turns," suggested Dilly, "because I'm sure we all have things we're dying to know."

"Excellent idea," agreed Ernie, "and since you thought of it, Dilly, you go first then we'll move round the table in a clockwise direction."

"Oh that's scary as it means I have to conjure the spirit up. Oh, well, best get on with it, so fingers on the glass everyone."

Everyone placed the forefinger of their right hand on the base of the up-turned glass.

Dilly half-closed her eyes and speaking slowly, her voice an octave lower than usual said: "Calling all spirits. Calling all spirits. Is there anyone there?" The glass moved slightly.

Dilly gasped. "I think someone's there. I can feel it in my bones."

"Try again," Amelia urged.

"Okay." Dilly took in a deep breath, "Calling all spirits, I ask again. Is there anyone there?" The glass suddenly slid across the table and stopped abruptly by the word, 'yes'. They all gasped.

"Well goodness me, I didn't expect a response as quick as that. Now it's my turn," Ernie straightened his shoulders and cleared his throat, "Spirit, are you a member of the Bray family?" After a quick wobble the glass moved to the 'yes'.

Freddie whose turn was next, felt his heart thumping in his chest. He knew what he wanted to ask but wasn't sure he wanted to know the answer. When he found his voice it was high-pitched. "Spirit, did you, or do you live in this house?" The glass moved to 'yes'.

In the candlelight it was difficult to see whose face was the paler, Freddie's or his godmother's.

Dotty next, aware it was down to her to establish the identity of the spirit, picked up her half-full wine glass in her free hand and drained it. "Spirit, spirit, are you…are you Frank?" The glass shot across the table towards the 'yes' rucking the cloth as it did so. Knowing her bottle of chardonnay was empty, Dotty refilled her glass to the brim with Ernie's elderberry wine, hoping to do so might stop her hands shaking.

Trying to act casually, John loosened the collar of his shirt. "Frank, I know it was a good few years ago, but do you remember your accident?"

The glass moved to 'yes'.

"My turn," Amelia shivered. "Frank, did you see who knocked you down?" The answer was 'yes'.

"Oh no. Back to me," whispered Dilly.

Dotty sniffed. "Hmm, I can smell lavender. It's really nice."

"So can I," John looked over his shoulder, "Is it the candles, Amelia?"

Amelia shook her head. "No, they're unscented."

Dilly pointed to the ceiling. "There's a bunch of dried flowers hanging up there on the beam by the fireplace. I picked them when I first arrived but they'd already gone to seed so the scent is very weak. In fact, I'm surprised you can smell it at all, John, because I can't and I'm nearer than you."

Amelia looked surprised. "I can smell it now and the scent is getting stronger."

"It is," agreed Dotty.

"Perhaps Elizabeth is here," chuckled Freddie, "remember what John said about lavender increasing clairvoyance or something like that. I expect she thinks we need a helping hand."

Dilly nervously looked over her shoulder. "That's not funny, Freddie."

"Well, I think it is," said Ernie, "even though I can't smell anything. Anyway, I think your imaginations are running away with you and rather than waffling on about lavender we ought to get back to Frank before he gets tired of waiting."

"Okay, I'll get back to him. Fingers back on the glass please," Dilly took in a deep breath. "Frank, who was it? Who was driving the car that knocked you down?"

All eyes were on the glass as it moved to the P and then the O. Back to the P and then the E. Y followed and then finally it moved back to the E. As Dilly screeched, "Popeye," the wine glass rolled to the edge of the table and fell onto Freddie's foot. Simultaneously, the framed photograph of Bert, Frank and their truck fell flat, face down, on the sideboard.

Chapter Thirteen

"Ha ha, very funny, so well done to whoever spelled out that." John chuckled and tears of laughter streamed down his face as he opened the third bottle of Ernie's elderberry wine.

Dotty sat motionless; her face devoid of colour. She clearly saw no reason to be flippant. "Well it wasn't me and I think it was for real otherwise why would the glass have rolled off the table like that?"

"And why did the photo topple over?" Amelia was equally spooked.

"I should imagine the glass rolled off because we all took our fingers away from it at the same time," reasoned Ernie.

"And as for the picture, it might not have been standing properly. Dilly was in a hurry when she dusted earlier today." Freddie like John thought someone was having a joke.

Dilly unsure what to think stood up and switched on the main light. She then blew out the candles. "Is anyone going to own up?"

No-one answered.

Amelia frowned. "Ernie, was it you? I know you liked Popeye when you were young and you still have several Popeye annuals."

Ernie shook his head. "No love it wasn't me but I have to admit I wish I'd thought of it."

Freddie held the wine glass up to the light to see if it was cracked. "Well, if it wasn't me, and it wasn't Ernie or

John it must be one of you females." Happy the glass was unscathed he stood it back on the table.

Dilly shook her head. "Well it certainly wasn't me and it obviously wasn't Dotty," She looked at her neighbour, "and I don't think it was you either, was it, Amelia?"

Amelia shook her head. "Definitely not. I'm still trembling."

Freddie was surprised to find himself feeling cold so he topped up the coke in the Truburn and opened its door to let out more warmth.

"That's better. I'm chilled to the marrow," admitted Dilly.

"Me too," said Dotty, "I feel light-headed too."

Amelia was sure she could smell lavender again but thought it best not to mention it.

"Where do we go from here?" Dilly needed answers.

"Well, as daft as it might sound, let's assume none of us manipulated the glass and concentrate instead on what Frank Bray's spirit told us," John found it difficult to hide the ridicule in his voice, "After all Popeye must mean something or why say it, spell it or whatever?"

Dotty frowned. "Well for a start off Popeye's not real and no-one surely would be called that. It's silly."

"Could be a nickname," reasoned Amelia.

Freddie nodded. "For someone who's a sailor, yes."

Dilly's jaw dropped. "Someone like Anthony Hammond, you mean. Remember he was in the Navy for twelve years or was it ten? Whatever, the length of time doesn't matter."

"But would Frank have known he'd been in the Navy?" Ernie asked.

"I don't see why not," said Dilly, "after all Bert knew."

"But he only met him a few hours before his death so why would he refer to him as Popeye? It's not like he was in uniform or anything like that," reasoned Freddie, "because by then he was a civilian."

Dilly drummed her fingers on the tablecloth. "Perhaps then it wasn't Anthony. Perhaps it was someone we're not even aware of who was in uniform on his way to or from work."

"Might not even have been a Royal Navy uniform," reasoned John, "It would all have happened very quickly and so the chap we're after could have been a fireman or even a police officer."

Dilly laughed. "No, surely a police officer would have stopped."

"So would a fireman," said Dotty.

Amelia shook her head. "I don't think it was either of them. Why would it be? We need someone with a motive."

"Not necessarily," said Dilly, "It could have been a genuine accident and the crime is that whoever the driver was, didn't stop."

"But Bert felt it might well have been Anthony," said John, "so I think pursuing him is our best bet. What's more, with Anthony there's the sailor connection."

Freddie sighed. "So having been all round the houses so to speak, we're back to square one. Looking for Anthony Hammond."

"But at least having spoken to Frank we have a bit of evidence now. Albeit rather dubious." Dilly found it hard to believe her own words.

"Yes, that's true," Amelia smiled as she watched Dotty's eyes roll and grow heavy until they closed and she flopped to one side, her head rested on Freddie's shoulder. "That'll be Ernie's elderberry wine. It has that effect on me. In fact it's a very useful nightcap."

Freddie moved his arm to make Dotty more comfortable. "What are we going to do with her? I mean, she's in no fit state to walk home and none of us are sober enough to drive."

Dilly stood up. "She'll have to stay here for the night. I'll make her a little bed in front of the stove." She left the room and returned shortly after with an eiderdown she'd seen behind the curtain and two blankets. She had also taken two of the four pillows from her own bed. Amelia helped her fold the double eiderdown in half and then spread it out in front of the Truburn. With pillows in place, Freddie and Ernie carefully lifted Dotty, laid her down on the makeshift bed, removed her shoes and covered her with the blankets.

Dilly looked down on Dotty sleeping peacefully. "I don't think she'll be jogging tomorrow."

"Or blogging hopefully," said John, "We don't want her telling people about tonight in case it's not Anthony Hammond we need to be going after."

"Good point," agreed Ernie, "Meanwhile I suggest we keep our options open and look into any people in the village who might have had a career that involved the wearing of a uniform back in the nineteen-seventies."

"Please don't think I'm being awkward," said Dilly, "but the person driving might not even have been from the village. He or she could just have been passing through."

"In which case we'll never get to the root of it," Amelia stood up, "Anyway, I don't know about you lot but I'm shattered and my bed's calling."

Everyone else agreed and the meeting was brought to a close.

The following morning, Freddie went to Hilltop Farm to finish his plastering job in the barn conversion leaving Dilly and Dotty sitting by the Truburn drinking coffee. Dotty had woken up at half past seven to hear the clock strike the half hour and rain lashing against the window panes. At first she'd had no idea where she was. When the room came into focus she'd groaned and the reason for her throbbing head became apparent.

Meanwhile, John, having promised to pursue his search further for Anthony Hammond on the off-chance he was responsible for Frank Bray's death, sat at the kitchen table in his cottage and Googled farms in the Plymouth area. When he had a list, he rang each in turn using a little poetic licence by saying he was looking into his family history and was wondering if they'd had a family in one of their tied cottages named Hammond. When he rang the third number on his list he was successful. For the friendly sounding man who answered said he remembered a Joan Hammond from when he was a boy. He never knew her husband because he'd died long before he was born. When asked what he remembered about Joan, he laughed and said the heavy cake she used to bake and he could see himself in her kitchen savouring every mouthful and washing it down with a glass of lemonade. John asked if he remembered her son, Anthony but sadly he didn't. Furthermore, Joan died when he was seven years old and then another couple moved into the furnished tied cottage. He'd love to be able to question his parents and grandparents who ran the farm back then but sadly all had since passed away. John thanked him for his help and then put down the phone. The call had tied up a dead end but at the same time achieved nothing. He wondered about contacting the Royal Navy but doubted they'd be able to help and even if they had a forwarding address, after he'd finished his length of service, the information would no doubt be confidential.

After phoning her boyfriend, Dotty stayed at Lavender Cottage for lunch and then slowly made her way home wearing a pair of Dilly's trainers and carrying her high heeled shoes inside a canvas bag. After she had gone,

Dilly feeling the need for fresh air, put on a warm coat, scarf and boots having decided to take a walk along the beach. As she locked the front door and dropped the key into her pocket, she looked at the lavender; it reminded her of the scent all but Ernie noticed the previous evening. Nonplussed as to why that might have been she made a mental note to cut back the plants on her return to encourage new growth in the spring.

A fresh south westerly wind blew up from the sea causing Dilly to put her hands deep inside her pockets as she crossed the road. On the other side she looked over the wall, the tide was out and so she'd be able to walk on the firm, compressed sand. With hands still in pockets she walked along the pavement until she reached one of the four sets of granite steps leading onto the beach. Holding the railings, she climbed down with care and when she stepped onto the shingle cast her eyes towards the top of the high wall. No longer was the street visible. Looking back and forth along the beach she saw no sign of life other than a solitary gull swooping above the waves. To maintain her balance she took her hands from her pockets and made her way down the pebbly incline towards the water's edge where large frothy waves tumbled onto the wet sand. As she reached the shoreline she looked back and was able to see the rooftops of Lavender and Yew Tree Cottages as in the picture taken many years before of Cyril and Carol on the beach. On turning back towards the sea she contemplated which way to go. To her left, sand stretched for half a mile and ended by caves and a mass of rocks jutting out into the sea. To her right the beach continued towards a headland and a manmade slipway for the launching of fishing boats. However, she had learned from Ernie that over the years the fishing fleet had diminished and most vessels now were rowing boats, Cornish pilot gigs, kayaks and boats for angling trips. Knowing the slipway led back to the road, Dilly opted for the latter. As she walked along the wet sand she felt alone in the world. Being late autumn there was little traffic on the road and it was difficult to imagine the beach busy with locals and holiday makers sunbathing and swimming: a scene having not arrived in the village until September she had yet to witness. For on the day she had viewed Lavender Cottage back in late June, the weather had been wet and the beach deserted.

When she reached the slipway she rested her hand on the side of a rowing boat, turned and looked back towards the distant rock formation. Smiling broadly she raised her hands and joyously shouted, "This is my home."

"And who could ask for more," laughed a voice from behind.

Feeling mortified, Dilly turned to see who had spoken. To her surprise it was the vicar with whom she had seen John speaking inside the Duck and Parrot." She held out her hand and smiled sweetly hoping he'd assume the redness of her cheeks was caused by the wind and not embarrassment. "Delighted to meet you, Vicar."

He took her hand and shook it warmly. "Likewise. We've not yet met but I believe you are the new owner of Albert's old house."

"Correct and my name is Dilly Granger."

"Well, as you've already realised, I'm Peter Goodman, vicar of this parish. I'm just about to take a walk along the beach. Care to join me, Dilly?"

"I'd be delighted." Dilly was happy to retrace her steps towards home.

"Good, it's nice to have someone to chat to. I'm a crusty old bachelor so the vicarage is very quiet. Except when Ivy is in, of course. She's my housekeeper and calls in every other day before she goes to work. She's a good woman and keeps me in order and up to date with happenings in the village. That's why I'm out here now, to stretch my legs. I've been in the attic, you see, because Ivy reminded me there was all sorts of stuff up there left by long departed clergy that might be of use to the auction," he laughed, "some no doubt from my own family."

"Your own family," repeated Dilly, "Why, were they clergy too?"

"My grandfather, James Keating was. He and my grandmother, Sybil, were here from 1944 to 1957."

"But your name's not Keating."

"No and that's because their daughter, Fiona, my mother, changed her name when she married my father, Gabriel Goodman."

"Of course, silly me. And Gabriel, was a wonderful name for the father of a vicar."

"It is but I'm not sure that he liked it. He wasn't a clergyman anyway. He was a banker. It was my mother who suggested I follow in her father's footsteps and I'm glad I did. Especially when the opportunity rose for me to come here. My grandparents always spoke of the village with great affection and I can see why."

"So can I, but what's this auction you mentioned in aid of?"

"It's to raise money for the homeless."

"That's a lovely idea. When is it?"

"The end of November. The date is yet to be confirmed."

"In that case I shall endeavour to find things to donate myself."

"Thank you, Dilly. We'd really appreciate that."

"So have you found anything exciting in the attic?"

"As a matter of fact I have. Toys. Lots of children's toys, some of which are a good age. There are a couple of old chests up there too but there's no rush so I'll leave going through them for another day. I find kneeling on old boards hard on the legs so don't want to do it all at once."

"Sounds exciting and we might be able to add a few toys as well because I remember Freddie saying there was a box of toy cars and what have you behind the curtain that we assume belonged to a young Bert. I must go through them."

"Behind the curtain?" the vicar seemed confused and so Dilly explained the situation.

"Anyway, will you be going to John's slide show next week?" Dilly asked as the vicar tried to visualise *behind the curtain*.

"Oh yes. I wouldn't miss that for anything. John is a wonderful rapporteur and the evenings are always very entertaining."

Chapter Fourteen

On Tuesday evening, Dilly changed into comfortable clothing to enable her arms to move freely and set off for the Duck and Parrot for the darts' team practice. As she approached the old inn she realised she'd yet to go inside without Freddie or the Trewellas to keep her company. Feeling a little apprehensive, she cautiously opened the door, hoping she wasn't too early and that someone she knew would be there. For although Dilly was by no means a shy woman she was not accustomed to going into public houses on her own. Once inside she bought herself a half pint of Guinness and made her way into the games room where to her relief Max and Dotty welcomed her warmly and introduced her to other team members. Most of the ladies were complete strangers of whom she had never heard but one name did stand out, Ivy. Ivy Richards who she felt sure was the vicar's housekeeper. Dilly, noting that Ivy was much nearer her own age than other team members, made a point of exchanging a few words throughout the evening and then when the practice concluded the two ladies sat together in the bar with drinks to get better acquainted. For Dilly was mesmerised by Ivy's Cornish accent and Ivy, in her mid-sixties, was fascinated by Dilly's pluck to have taken on Lavender Cottage at the age of seventy-two.

"And I hear you've found Bert's old Harley," said Ivy, "and in the pantry of all places. Mind you, it were always inferred that Bert was a bit odd, but I liked him and I liked his bike."

"You remember it then?"

"Oh yes. Not only do I remember it," Ivy glanced over her shoulders as though checking to see if anyone was listening, "but I rode on it."

Dilly's jaw dropped. "You rode on it."

"Yes, and it made me as proud as punch. You see I was only ten at the time."

"Ten!"

Ivy lowered her voice. "As you can imagine it was a few years ago but I remember it like it were yesterday. I was up at the rec. I don't know if you've been there but it's a good-sized field not far from the school and has always been popular with kids. Anyway, on the day in question I was up there on my own and I was down in the dumps because my world had fallen apart. My then best friend told me she had another best friend, you see. I was sitting on top of the slide, crying when Bert rode onto the field on his bike. He stopped by the roundabout, switched off the engine and lit a cigarette. He didn't see me at first but when he did he got off his bike walked over and asked if I was alright. I told him I was but then changed my mind and told him about Julie and her new best friend. He was very sympathetic but at the same time seemed amused. I remember his smile. He told me to cheer up and then asked if I'd like a ride on his bike." She chuckled, "He took me for a spin twice round the field. Of course that made me quite popular at school. I mean, having a bike like Bert's bike was the aspiration of most of the boys. Mind you I didn't tell Mum or Dad and if they ever heard on the grapevine they never mentioned it to me."

"So what happened to Julie?"

A mischievous grin stretched across Ivy's face. "The new best friend moved away. Julie didn't know it but she was only here temporarily anyway. After she'd gone Julie asked me to be her best friend again. Needless to say I said yes because I liked her and we're still friends to this day. Although she lives in Truro now so I don't see a great deal of her."

"So it all ended happily ever after."

"You could say that."

"So what's the vicar like? I met him briefly the other day and we walked along the beach together and he seemed really nice."

"He's lovely but a bit untidy. What he really needs is a wife but I get the impression he's quite happy on his own."

"Is he Cornish? I know his grandparents were in the village some time ago but that doesn't mean they were Cornish and I didn't detect a local accent," Dilly smiled, "not like yourself."

"Do you know, I'm not sure. As you say his grandfather was vicar here in the forties and fifties but they could have come from anywhere. I shall endeavour to find out."

"And are you and your ancestors lifelong natives of this village?"

"Very much so. In fact my great grandmother was a Jago. Victoria Jago."

"Jago! Really! So was she by any chance related to Bert's grandmother, Elizabeth Bray? She was a Jago before she married George Bray."

"I know and she certainly was. Victoria was Elizabeth's younger sister. I think that's why Bert took me for a spin on his bike. He knew I was a distant relative but didn't know how and neither did I."

"Well, I never. I'm at a loss for words."

Ivy's eyes twinkled. "How about saying yes to another drink?"

"Sounds like a good idea but I can't drink any more Guinness. I don't have the capacity." Dilly drained her glass and stood, "So I'll move on to wine. Same again for you?"

"Yes, but I was going to get them. That's why I suggested it."

"Another time perhaps," Dilly picked up Ivy's empty glass and made her way to the bar.

At half past ten the two ladies said goodbye to team members still there and left for home. Ivy admitted she would have liked to stay longer but she cooked breakfast for the vicar on Monday, Wednesday and Friday mornings at eight o'clock prompt before going on to the off licence where she had a part-time job.

After leaving the pub they walked down the road together chatting like lifelong friends. Opposite Chapel Terrace, Ivy stopped walking. "Well, this is as far as I go. I live over the road."

"In Chapel Terrace?"

"No, in one of the bungalows in a cul-de-sac behind. You can't quite see it from here."

They crossed the road together. "Now that's interesting. I mean, being so near, did you hear anything on the night Frank Bray was knocked down in the hit and run?"

Ivy shook her head. "No, simply because I was out with my then boyfriend who I might add married someone else a long time ago. Dad wasn't in either. He was at the pub."

"And your mother?"

"Mum died a few years before so it was just me and Dad and with no siblings and the fact my marriage failed, it's just me now."

"You've been married then. I won't be indelicate and ask what happened."

"It wouldn't be indelicate to ask and everyone knows anyway. No, after five years of marriage my hubby ran off with the milkman."

"The milkman! Oh, oh, I see."

Ivy chuckled. "I'm pulling your leg. It was actually the postman."

Dilly jaw dropped and clearly confused she was unable to think of an appropriate response.

"I think you're shocked but don't be. We're still the best of friends and I'm happy for them both. Anyway, it was a long time ago."

"Do they live in the village? Your ex and the postman, I mean."

"No, they live in town but we keep in touch and I visit them from time to time."

"Good. It'd be silly to bear a grudge."

"Very true, and would I be right in thinking you've never married?"

"You would but I'm not on my own as my godson lives with me."

"Yes, I've heard all about him from various folks. In fact a lot of my contemporaries wish they were twenty years younger."

Dilly smiled, glad to hear Freddie was popular. "Anyway, if I don't see you before, Ivy, I'll see you at next week's darts practice."

"Oh. Aren't you going to John's history chat tomorrow night?"

"Goodness me, yes, I'd forgotten that. I take it you'll be there."

"Definitely. Meanwhile, I'll see if I can turn up any pictures of my great granny, Victoria."

"Yes, please do. I'd love to see if she looks anything like the picture we have of Elizabeth," Dilly frowned, "It's just a thought. But Elizabeth Bray nee Jago was obviously your great aunt so I wonder, can you read tealeaves?"

Ivy threw back her head and laughed. "I've never tried, Dilly. I've never tried."

The following morning, after Freddie had gone to work, Dilly, prompted by her chat with Ivy the previous evening, decided to look behind the curtain for the box of toys Freddie had found in order to see if any were suitable for the church auction mentioned by the vicar. As she knelt down on the floor it suddenly occurred to her that Bert did have a living relative after all. Ivy. But then she reasoned they were so far removed that to have made Ivy a beneficiary when there would no doubt be other distant relatives out there, would have been unfair. Then there was Anthony Hammond. Surely he should have been part of the equation. A vision of the photo depicting the Hammond family on the beach flashed across her mind. Did Bert's elusive cousin have any offspring? If he had then he or she could or should have been in line to inherit Lavender Cottage. "Oh well," she muttered to herself, "What's done is done and it's too late to make amends now. I really would like to know if Anthony was involved in his uncle's death though."

After moving several objects around she found the box of toys, took it into the living room and tipped its contents onto the rug in front of the Truburn. There was just about every mode of transport you could imagine. Tractors, vans, trucks, diggers, bicycles, a fire engine, buses, boats, military vehicles, an ambulance, several motorbikes, a police car and a train engine but no coaches or track. Several of the vehicles were battered and dented. A few were still in their boxes. Dilly divided them into two heaps. The first, of toys she deemed too damaged to sell and the other of toys in a good condition. As she picked up the model ambulance, the back doors flew open. Instinctively Dilly looked inside. To her surprise she saw a matchbox. Intrigued as to why it might be there, she carefully withdrew it. Inside, wrapped in a crumpled piece of Christmas paper, lay a half-crown coin. Dilly placed it on the palm of her hand. The coin was dated 1935 and must have been hidden for at least fifty years because in the early nineteen seventies the country's currency had changed to decimal and sterling was phased out. Why it was hidden there she had no idea but felt it only right that it be returned to its hiding place and the vehicle in question must not be amongst those she selected for the auction. However, curious to know if other vehicles housed hidden treasures she went through every one but all were empty. As she returned the box of vehicles to be retained behind the curtain, a bundle of wire coat hangers caught her eye. "Aha," she muttered, "Ideal, I have a little job for one of you." She pulled one from the bundle, took it into the living room and placed it on the table while she went to a drawer of miscellaneous objects in the kitchen cabinet in search of a pair of wire cutters. Consequently the following morning when Freddie arose and entered the living room he found his godmother kneeling in front of the Truburn, its door wide open as she toasted crumpets on the glowing coke.

"Whatever is that contraption you're holding?" he laughed.

"It's my new toasting fork. I tried using a dining fork yesterday but it burned my hand. This is ideal. I made it from an old wire coat hanger. Make do and mend. That's the motto in this house, Freddie. Make do and mend."

Because November was a quiet month, especially during the week, the licensees of the Duck and Parrot were happy, as in previous years, to close the dining room for John Martin's history evening. For the event was usually well attended, created a jovial atmosphere and most of the enthusiasts had at least one drink. Some even arrived early and had a meal in the bar.

John arrived at the pub just after six-thirty, set up his equipment and then took a seat at the end of the bar with a pint of cider to await the arrival of his audience. By seven o'clock the bar was filling up and so the dining room door was opened and people made their way to the room where they seated themselves around tables or on chairs in rows facing the screen. Dilly, Freddie, Amelia and Ernie were amongst them, as were Dotty and her boyfriend, Gerry. To Freddie's disappointment, he learned from Dotty that Max had decided to give the evening a miss; her mother had a nasty bout of gastric flu and Max didn't want to spread germs.

At seven-thirty as the last person entered the dining room and took their seat, John asked Gerry sitting on the back row to switch off the lights. As Gerry reached for the switch, the door flew open and the vicar tumbled into the room seemingly out of breath. In his hand he held a large wooden box. "Look what I found in the attic, John," he puffed. "It was in one of the chests. I'd have been here earlier but couldn't leave it because I was intrigued as to what was inside but couldn't find the key. Found it eventually though and so glad I persevered." He opened up the box. Inside were row upon row of neatly packed slides. "Needless to say I've not had a chance to look at them and I don't have a projector anyway." He handed the box to John and then flopped down in the nearest chair by Ivy who tutted when she saw the cobwebs on his dusty trousers.

"Now this could be interesting," John took out a slide and held it over the light from the projector, "Looks like it's taken inside the church. I'll run through the ones I've already selected and then we'll have a look at these during the second half."

The first half of the evening involved slides John had taken himself since the day when he first took up photography back in 1985. Some he had shown before especially ones of the deep snow the village encountered in January 1987. Others were more recent.

During the interval John mounted the vicar's slides onto the tray ready to be viewed when all had refilled their glasses and had returned to their seats.

The first slides were taken inside the church and depicted Christmas, Easter and a harvest festival. The next were of fishing boats.

"Well I never," John chuckled, "For those of you that don't know, that's me and my brother Bruce coming in on Sassy Sal. It was probably taken in the seventies."

"Lovely picture," said Ernie.

"Lovely boat," said a voice from the back of the room.

John turned round. "And again, to those of you that don't know, the voice at the back belongs to Zippy Lugg. Zippy bought Sassy Sal off me when I retired."

"Do you miss fishing?" Dilly noted he'd spoken of his erstwhile boat with affection.

"Yes, of course. When you do something for as long as I did, it's hard to let go. Luckily Zippy is happy to take me out once in a while and for that I'm extremely grateful."

"I gotta look after you, boss and it's good to pick your brains."

"So where does your brother live?" Freddie realised he not yet encountered him.

"Bruce lives at The Elms. That's sheltered accommodation for the elderly. He has a smashing flat there and seems very happy. When his wife died he was keen to give up his home and move there for the company. I told him if it's company he's after he could move in with me but he wasn't keen and wanted to be independent. I could see his point and I must admit my house has small windows and is a bit dull and pokey, whereas his flat is bright, spacious and more importantly lovely and warm."

"Certainly is," agreed Zippy, "my gran lives at the Elms too and she's as happy as Larry."

"Yes, Bruce often has a chat with her. Anyway, back to the slides, I think."

The next one raised a lot of laughter. It was the cast of a pantomime.

"Good grief," said John, "How embarrassing. This would have been way back in 1957. The pantomime was put on by the church and in case you're wondering, it's Cinderella."

"So who's who?" asked the vicar, "I don't see anyone I recognise."

"Well, Cinderella was played by Carol. Your mum, Emma." He nodded towards the post mistress.

"So, it is. I must admit I didn't recognise her at first but then I didn't know her back then."

"Not surprised, she'd have only been fifteen." John sounded wistful, "We were all young then."

"Are you there then, John?" asked Dilly.

"I am indeed. I'm one of the ugly sisters. The other was Godfrey Lane who sadly is no longer with us. As you can see I was a puny youth. It wasn't 'til I started fishing that I developed any muscles and had a growth spurt."

"Who's Prince Charming?" Gerry asked, "Because whoever she is, she has a smashing pair of legs."

"Now that's Sybil Keating," laughed John, "Your grandmother, Vicar."

The vicar's jaw dropped.

"She was a good sort and a smashing woman, Peter. We all adored her. In fact the pantomime was her idea. She wanted us to have some fun and raise money for the church roof at the same time. We thought it a wonderful idea but said she'd have to be Prince Charming because of her long legs. It was wonderful and really brought us all together."

John moved on to the next slide. "Well, I never. This is one for you Dilly. The lady there playing the piano for the show is Bert's mum, Ethel Bray. And a damn good pianist she was too."

"So I've heard."

John moved on to the last slide. "Oh, my goodness, I'd forgotten what a good sport he was." The slide was of a bulky man dressed in a long flowy dress. He wore a shoulder length dark curly wig, was heavily made up and held a glittery wand in his right hand. "Our fairy godmother. Of course the part is usually played by a female but Frank wanted to do it and he was perfect."

"Frank. That's Frank," spluttered Dilly, "but I was of the impression he was bad-tempered, mean and unsociable."

"In later years perhaps," said Julian, the architect, "but I recall my late father saying that in his heyday, Frank Bray was the life and soul of the party."

Chapter Fifteen

At the end of November the church held its auction and to the delight of those involved raised a considerable amount of money. Dilly in particular was happy because Bert's toy cars sold to a collector who knowing their worth made a substantial donation on top of the price raised through bidding.

As the days grew shorter and the month gave way to December, all thoughts of seeking justice for Frank Bray faded to be replaced by plans for Christmas. Behind the curtain, Dilly had found a box of Christmas decorations and said rather than buy new ones she'd put them up hopefully to recreate how the house might have looked in days gone by. But that was a job for later. Before they bought a tree and put up decorations, she and Freddie had already decided to tidy up the front room and make use of it during the festive season when at some point they hoped to invite around newly made friends.

One morning after Freddie had gone off to work on a new job, Dilly put on her trainers and waited outside for Dotty so the two might jog around the village together. As usual Dotty arrived on time and they carried on along the main street. As they approached the church a white transit van pulled away.

"Ah, that'll be Reg. No doubt having just erected Bert's memorial stone. Someone said the other day it was due any time now."

"When you say Bert, I assume you mean Bert Bray."

"I do. Apparently he had the headstone made years ago and it's been in Reg's yard ever since."

"Reg being?"

"Reg Rogers. A memorial stonemason. It's a family affair and they've been going for a hundred years or more."

"Oh dear. I don't like the idea of arranging my own memorial stone. It's something I'd rather not think about but then I suppose Bert had to do it himself because there would be no-one else to do it for him. Him being the last of the Brays."

Dotty smiled. "Well we thought he was but now we know he has a mysterious cousin called Anthony. Or should I say elusive cousin."

"It certainly seems that way," Dilly slowed, "How about we take a detour round the churchyard and see what the headstone says?"

"I think that's an excellent idea."

When they reached the gate Dotty lifted the heavy latch. They then went inside and jogged along the gravel path. They found Bert's grave at the far end of the churchyard in what was clearly an extension out into a meadow. Dilly read out the inscription.

Here lies the body of Albert George Bray. (Bert)
Born April 3rd 1935
Died when St Peter called out his name.
Only son of Francis (Frank) Bray and Ethel Bray nee Rowe.
The last of a family of builders
who dearly loved Trenwalloe Sands.
United and at rest.

Dotty smiled. "Dear old Bert. I do like 'Died when St. Peter called out his name.' I hardly knew him but it's said he had a great sense of humour and of course he wouldn't have known his expiry date when the inscription was done. Although I suppose it could have been added later."

Dilly ran her hand along the polished granite stone. "I agree but it seems so sad that Bert having written his own obituary means it doesn't say, in loving memory, dearly beloved, much treasured or anything sentimental like that."

"No it doesn't. That is sad. Perhaps we could put some flowers on his grave to show that someone cares."

"Or a wreath. A Christmas holly wreath. That's what we'll do, in fact why don't we make one?"

Dotty raised her hand. "Good idea and I know where there's a holly bush with lots of berries."

"You do. Where?"

Dotty took out her phone and pressed a number. "Hilltop Farm where Max lives. I'm just ringing her to make sure it's okay."

Max not only said it was alright for them to take holly, but suggested they come to the farmhouse where she and her mother would help make a wreath not just for Bert but for their respective doors also. Dilly was delighted. Having heard from Freddie of the long ago engagement between Bert and Max's great aunt she was keen to see the farm and visualise where Bert's one time sweetheart had lived.

As they turned to leave the graveyard, the vicar's car pulled up outside the gates.

"Morning ladies," he waved as he locked his car.

"Morning, Vicar," Dotty returned his wave as the clergyman walked towards them, "Have you met Dilly yet?"

"I have indeed on several occasions the last time being the auction," He held out his hand, "Lovely to see you again, Dilly?"

She shook the proffered hand, "Likewise and we've just stopped by to see, well, you know, to see Bert's memorial stone."

"Yes, dear Bert. I regret to say I knew him only by sight, but the money from the sale of his house, your house, will greatly benefit the community. The church wardens and I had a meeting the other day and we've agreed the money must go towards a hall that can be used by all. I'm told there used to be a village hall where the surf board shop is but it was demolished in the early seventies because it was in a bad state of repair and also built of mundic block."

"Mundic block?" puzzled Dilly, "what on earth is that?"

"Mundic is a Cornish word," said the vicar, "I know but only because I looked it up. The blocks in question were used for construction during the first half of the last century and unlike the blocks used today, mundics were made of mine waste and aggregate, such as sand, sulphite minerals, furnace residue or flint. I'm told walls built of mundic are as hard as iron and prone to be damp probably due to the salt content in the sand taken from beaches."

"Interesting," mused Dilly. "I wonder why they didn't rebuild the hall though."

"Money, I suppose, although someone said with the ever growing population of the village the original site was too small. No room for parking either and that's essential in this day and age."

"Very true," Dilly agreed.

"So where will the new hall be?" Dotty was keen to learn first-hand.

"The church owns the large field adjoining this graveyard. If we can get planning permission it'll be just over there." He waved his hand towards the green open space, "And if it gets built, we'll name it after Bert and call it Albert's Hall."

Dilly clapped her hands together. "Wonderful. I do hope it goes ahead."

"Me too," agreed Dotty. "Meanwhile, we're off to Hilltop Farm to get holly to make Bert a wreath. We feel sorry for him, you see, having had to organise his own headstone and want to let it be known that he is missed."

"A lovely idea," agreed the vicar, "It's a shame there's no date on his stone but he insisted it read as it does. Mind you, I'll always remember the date because he died on my fiftieth birthday."

The Hilltop farmhouse kitchen was huge. Beneath a large, stripped pine table in the centre of the room, a floral rug lay on a flagstone floor. A functional, well maintained Cornish Range stood in the inglenook fireplace and cooking utensils of all shapes and sizes hung from wooden beams along with bunches of herbs and strings of garlic. Beneath a large window with views over the farmyard, a Belfast sink sat twixt two wooden draining boards and beside a radiator in the corner of the room, a black Labrador dog lay curled up on an old tartan blanket.

"Hmm, something smells nice," said Dilly, after greetings were exchanged and she'd learned that Max's mother was called Helen.

"Pasties," said Max, "Mum likes to keep her hand in and makes them at least twice a week."

Helen glanced at the clock as she loaded cooking utensils into the dishwasher. "Well, if you pop out and grab a few boughs of holly now, by the time you get back they'll be ready and have cooled a little."

"Sounds good," said Dotty, "I've always room for a pasty."

Max took a jacket from a hook on the back of the kitchen door. "I'll go with you and to save time we'll take the Land Rover. Holly is too prickly to carry far and the track's a bit muddy in places."

"And while you've gone I'll look out ribbons, wires and so forth. I'll also get some moss from the path by the pond and collect some of the cones that are under the fir trees." Helen kicked off her slippers and put on a pair of sturdy shoes.

Sensing people were going outside, the dog rose and looked expectantly from one person to another.

Helen patted his head. "You can come with me, Stanley. You could do with the exercise but we don't want you trampling over holly as you'd likely get hurt."

When Dilly, Dotty and Max arrived back, Helen had taken the pasties from the oven and on the table, colourful ribbons, wires, moss, cones and silver spray paint were spread out on newspaper.

"Well done, Mum," Max and Dotty dropped bunches of holly alongside everything else and Dilly put down strands of ivy.

"Shall we eat first or would you rather wait?" Helen nodded towards a worktop where the pasties cooled on a wire rack.

"I'm starving," said Max, "Been up since six. What about you two?"

Dotty and Dilly agreed they'd be happy to eat first.

"Ideal," Helen pushed the foliage and other wreath making paraphernalia to one end of the table and placed four plates at the other end. "Sit down, ladies."

After lunch Helen made tea for everyone and the ladies set to making wreaths. While they worked they talked about life on the farm, the weather, village activities and briefly even politics. Dilly wanted to ask about Max's great aunt who she calculated would be Helen's aunt but thought to do so would be tactless. She was delighted therefore when Helen asked about Bert.

"I've just realised you never knew Bert, did you, Dilly?"

"Sadly no but at the same time I feel I know him and the rest of the family quite well because many of their possessions are still in the house."

"Yes, Max told me that was the case and finding the motorbike must have been a great surprise to you. It certainly got tongues wagging in the village."

"It was more of a shock than a surprise. In my wildest dreams I'd never have expected to find a motorbike in the pantry."

"I suppose not," Helen stood to collect the empty mugs, "Max also said she'd told your wonderful godson about her great aunt's liaison with Bert, albeit many years ago. Such a sad tale."

"It is, and would I be right in thinking Max's great aunt would be your aunt, Helen?"

"Only by marriage. I was a Triggs before I became a Pascoe. Bert's ex-love, Mary was my husband's father's sister and her married name was Trelawney. Her husband Edward was a school teacher in Penzance, or was it Truro? I can never remember."

Dotty laughed. "Ouch. I don't think I'll try and get my head round that bit of your family history."

"Best not too," agreed Dilly, "Fathoming out family history can be very complicated. As is the case with Bert. Well, actually no, his family isn't complicated at all, is it? It's just we can't track down his Aunt Joan's son, Anthony."

"Even that sounds complicated to me," laughed Max, "and for the record, Mum, Edward taught in Truro."

When the wreaths were finished Max hung one of them on the front door of the farmhouse and after saying their farewells, Dotty and Dilly carried the other three back into the village where they stopped at the church and put one on Bert's grave beneath the newly erected memorial stone. So they could chat, they walked the rest of the way to Lavender Cottage where Dotty took her leave and jogged home. Dilly then screwed a hook onto the front door and hung her wreath. Pleased with her effort, she stood back to admire her handiwork. "All in all, a good day's work," she said.

Freddie arrived home from work later than usual and when he did get in, a broad grin was stretched across his face.

"What are you so happy about?" Dilly smiled herself, always glad to see evidence that he was enjoying life in Cornwall.

"Jim Blake, the retired fisherman I'm currently doing a job for heard me singing today. I didn't even know he was there. He popped out, you see, to post a parcel and I didn't hear him come back. Anyway, he said I had a great voice and I ought to join the village's male voice choir. That's why I'm late. He took me round to meet Orville King; he's the choir leader. Orville got me to do a bit of singing, liked what he heard and I'm in."

"That's wonderful. I've always said you've a smashing voice, so it's fantastic to hear you're going to put it to good use." Dilly stood and took the kettle from the Truburn knowing he'd be ready for a mug of tea, "So where does this choir perform?"

"All sorts of places. Pubs, clubs, churches and chapels, organised dinners, regattas, agricultural shows and they even do the occasional concert." Freddie sat down, removed his boots and warmed his feet by the fire.

"Sounds lovely. How many members does it have?" Dilly handed Freddie his tea and then sat back down.

"Can't answer that one because at the moment I've only met Jim and Orville. Having said that there was a photo of the choir on Orville's mantelpiece and I'd estimate there would have been about twenty blokes on it."

"So you'll be off practising now I suppose."

"Yes, and I've got lots of words to learn. Orville gave me a list of songs they do and some of the Cornish ones I've never even heard of. So that I can catch up I'm going round to his place a couple of times a week to learn the tunes and then the whole choir rehearse once a week. If I can get up to scratch quite quickly I might even be able to sing with them on some of their Christmas gigs."

"You're going to be a busy boy then and I'm really glad for you."

"Thanks, and thanks for giving me the chance to start a new life. I don't think I've been as happy for years."

"I'm glad to hear it. So where do Orville King and Jim Blake live? I assume they're both in the village."

"They are. Orville lives on the Buttercup Field estate. He's only been there a couple of years and before that lived in the family home with his older sister who was a widow. When she died he thought the house was too big for one and so sold it and bought a two bedroomed bungalow."

"Probably near Cyril then. How about Jim?"

"Jim lives at Chapel Terrace and of course that's where I'm doing jobs for him and his wife, Susan. Which reminds me, he was telling me earlier that he used to live here. Not in this house, I might add, but part of what's now Yew Tree Cottage."

"Really, when was that?"

"In the nineteen-fifties. He was only a boy and they left there when he was eight so he doesn't remember it that well. But he reckons they were the last people to live there until Cyril bought it and the one next door and knocked the two into one. At the time they were living there his dad worked for the Brays and so I suppose that's why they got the house to rent. Apparently Jim's dad and Frank didn't get on all that well, but his mum and Ethel were quite chummy. Jim's words, not mine. The family were only there for a few years though because when Jim's granny, his dad's mum, died, she left her house in Chapel Terrace to him. They moved soon after and then Jim's dad went to work at the local builders' merchants."

"And is that the same house in Chapel Terrace where Jim's living now?"

"That's right."

"It's funny isn't it that we get conflicting reports about Frank. I mean, it seems some people thought he was fun and other didn't like him at all."

Freddie shrugged his shoulders. "I suppose you could say that about anyone. One man's meat is another man's poison and all that."

"True."

"And I suppose you're wondering if you would have liked him."

Dilly looked over the rim of her glasses. "Since when have you been into mind reading?"

"I expect Elizabeth put the thought into my head," With a chuckle he cast a cheeky grin at the erstwhile mistress of Lavender Cottage. "Anyway, what have you been up to today?"

Dilly, happily told of her jog with Dotty, Bert's memorial stone and the trip to Hilltop Farm.

Chapter Sixteen

On Christmas Eve, Dilly, Freddie, Amelia and Ernie went to the Duck and Parrot where the Trenwalloe Sands Singers were due to perform at some point during the evening. Because he still had many words to learn, Freddie was not confident enough to join in and so had opted to watch them instead.

"Who's that dashingly handsome young man serving on the bar with Gail and Robert?" Dilly asked Amelia as they took seats around a square table while Ernie and Freddie went to the bar for drinks.

"That's Dylan. He's their son."

Dilly removed her coat and sat down. "Really! How come I've not seen him here before?"

"He only helps out when it's busy in the winter. In the summer he doesn't have the time. He gives surfing lessons to locals and holiday makers and also works as a lifeguard on the beach."

"I see. So does he live here in the pub?"

Amelia shook her head. "No, he lives with his girlfriend, Jess. She's an estate agent and they have a little cottage at the far side of the village." She nodded her head towards the end of the bar, "That's Jess sitting on a barstool next to Dotty."

"Wow, what a tan. She looks as though she's into surfing too."

"She is but I think this time of year the tan has a helping hand."

"That's the trouble, isn't it? A tan looks great for a couple of weeks and then fades rapidly. Not that I've ever been a sun worshipper. Too fair-skinned, I'm afraid."

When the men returned with the drinks Dilly patted Freddie's arm. "Freddie love, please don't think you have to stay with us. As much as we enjoy your company, I'd much rather you were with people of your own age, so why don't you go and join Dotty and Jess?"

"Jess isn't my age she's only twenty-six," Freddie sat down, "besides two's company and three's a crowd."

"How come you know Jess?" Dilly asked.

"Because she's Jim's granddaughter and she popped in to see him a week or so ago when I was working at his place and Jim introduced us. Jim of course being the chap who encouraged me to join the choir. Anyway, I told him he didn't look old enough to have a grown-up granddaughter and he said he was seventy-two and so more than old enough and Jess was only twenty-six."

Heads automatically turned every time the door of the pub opened and the next to arrive were Max and her mother.

"Helen," called Dilly, "How lovely to see you again."

"You too," she pecked Dilly on the cheek.

"Do you mind if I join you, then Max can go and chat with Dotty without feeling she's abandoned me?"

"Of course," Dilly turned to Freddie, "You can have Freddie's seat and he can join Max with Dotty and Jess."

"Yes, come on, Freddie," Max pulled Freddie from his seat, the two then went with arms linked towards the end of the bar.

"They make a lovely couple," Helen sat down and unzipped her jacket, "I'd love Max to settle down but she's very headstrong and insists she's happy to be a singleton. I'm sure she'll regret it when I'm gone though. It can get very lonely up at the farm especially this time of year when it's dark so early."

Dilly shuddered. "I can imagine. Your farm is very isolated."

"Doesn't the fact that Dotty and Gerry seem very happy together make her want a partner?" asked Amelia.

"I don't think so. In fact she said only the other day that it'd be a nightmare for Dotty if Gerry got promoted and spent even more time working than he does now."

"Yes, I can see that. Unsociable hours too as with any job that needs twenty-four hour cover."

"And stress if and when they get a high profile case to solve," Dilly added, "no doubt made worse by pressure from the media, government and the chief officer, superintendent or whatever he or she is called these days."

"Chief constable, I think," pondered Amelia, "but I may well be wrong."

"Do they live together? Dotty and Gerry I mean," asked Dilly.

Helen shook her head. "Not at the moment. Gerry has his own place over the road so very handy for the pub. Max reckons he'll probably move in with Dotty soon though as they seem to be getting quite serious. And if that happens he'll rent his cottage out."

A little later Dilly bought a round of drinks and Amelia helped her carry them.

"Cyril's down the other end of the bar with his daughter Emma and her chap," said Amelia, as she placed the full glasses on the table, "You must tell him how much you've enjoyed looking at the house plans if you get the chance, Ernie."

"I'll do that next time I pop to the Gents."

"Cyril loves to hear the choir," sighed Helen, "He was a member for a while but gave up when he turned eighty. Said his voice wasn't as good as it used to be and he found it difficult to remember the words of new songs."

"That's a shame," empathised Dilly. "You know our Freddie's joined them but he's not performed with them yet because he's not familiar with their entire repertoire."

"So Max said and he seems to be settling well into the Cornish way of life."

"He is and I'm sure he has no regrets."

As the evening went on, choir members and their families began to arrive and at half past nine they sang their first song. Much to Dilly's delight it was Mary's Boy Child; the years disappeared and Dilly saw herself as a little girl, with her mother playing Harry Belafonte's much-treasured version of the song on her old record player.

The choir's performance was greatly appreciated and when they finished with a moving rendition of Silent Night, a collection was made for a local charity. As choir members were plied with drinks with the licensee's compliments, Freddie brought Orville King, the choir leader, over to meet his godmother.

"Charmed, I'm sure," Orville kissed her hand and took a bow.

"I'm flattered. Do sit down, Mr King," Dilly waved to the seat Helen had vacated when she'd gone to speak with an old school friend.

"Orville, please. Mr King is far too formal."

"And you must call me Dilly."

Orville sat down. "So, Dilly, you live in Bert's old place. How are you liking it?"

"Very much. It's a wonderful spot and the house oozes character. Admittedly it'll be nice when we have a bathroom installed but we're able to manage for now, thanks to Amelia and Ernie."

"Are they alright as neighbours then?" Orville winked at the Trewellas.

"Couldn't ask for better."

"And we're happy with Dilly and Freddie as neighbours too," chuckled Ernie. "There's not been a dull moment since they arrived."

"So I've heard. And you found Bert's old bike. Fancy that."

Ernie chuckled. "Yes, that was a turn up for the book. It's a beauty too."

"You must pop in and see it if ever you're passing," said Dilly. "It's looking quite spectacular now Ernie has tinkered with it and cleaned it up."

"I might just do that. Never been a great fan of motorbikes but I know it was a beast and I can still see and hear Bert roaring through the village on it ignoring the speed restrictions."

Dilly tutted. "Did you know Bert well?"

"I knew him fairly well but he was ten years older than me so we weren't at school together. He was a bit of a tearaway in his youth but in later years kept himself to himself especially after he lost his mum and dad. Very sad that was."

"So I take it you were living in the village then?"

"Yes, been here all my life as were my parents before me. In fact I wouldn't live anywhere else."

"I can understand that."

"So you must have been around on the night Frank was killed in the hit and run," said Amelia.

"I was. In fact I was here in the pub having a drink with some of my mates. I remember Frank arriving. He was in a foul mood and seemed to want to argue with anyone and everyone. Then of course the more he drank the worse he got. In the end the then landlord, umm, damn, I can't remember his name, took Frank to one side and asked him to keep his voice down. After that, Frank polished off his pint, banged the glass down on the bar and stormed out slamming the door behind him. Needless to say we all heaved a sigh of relief when he'd gone but none of us imagined we'd never see him again. Poor sod."

"So would I be right in thinking he probably upset a few people that night?" Dilly asked.

"Yes, just about everyone in the pub. We never did find out why he was in such a foul mood. Someone said a family member had turned up and upset him but I don't know who it could have been and no more was said. As for who knocked him down, well, that's anybody's guess."

Chapter Seventeen

Christmas Day dawned dry, bright and sunny. Dilly and Freddie enjoyed a quiet morning chilling out, watching TV and trying not to eat too much. John called in briefly at midday to wish them a happy Christmas on his way to Elm House to join his brother, Bruce and other residents for Christmas dinner. After he left, dressed in their finery, Dilly and Freddie joined Amelia and Ernie for dinner at Yew Tree Cottage. Earlier in the month, Amelia and Dilly had both expressed the desire to play hostess on the big day and so in order to decide where the meal should take place they tossed a coin for it and Amelia won.

The day, although quiet, was enjoyed by all. They ate at one-thirty, watched a film in the afternoon and then while the senior citizens dozed by the fire, Freddie took Oscar for a walk around the village.

The weather on Boxing Day was cold, dry and frosty and so shortly after breakfast, Dilly, Freddie, Amelia and Ernie, wrapped up in warm clothing, went for a stroll along the beach with Oscar. There was not a breath of wind, the tide was out and the water flat like a millstone. At the far end of the beach they walked up the slipway and made their way over the road and through the village back streets until having completed a circle they arrived home where, in return for the Trewellas' hospitality the previous day, Dilly insisted her neighbours join them at Lavender Cottage for refreshments.

"Tea or coffee?" Freddie reached for the kettle on the Truburn as everyone removed their outer garments.

All asked for coffee.

After Dilly made up the fire, she went into the under stairs cupboard and came out with a cake tin containing homemade mince pies. She took plates from the kitchen cabinet and then offered the tin around. "Let's go into the front room. Freddie lit a fire in the stove this morning and it's really cosy in there."

All agreed, picked up their refreshments, and made their way into the front room.

A rustle of coloured foil strips hanging from a wire circle greeted them as they entered the room. "You've put decorations up," said Amelia, approvingly.

"Yes," said Dilly, "and apart from the Christmas tree which Freddie bought at the post office, all decorations including the ones on the tree, were in a box behind the curtain."

The Christmas tree stood on the wooden top of a glass fronted display cabinet situated between the two windows. A twisted, ruched, rainbow-coloured strip of crepe paper ran along the knobbly beam. A small nativity scene sprinkled with glitter took centre stage on the mantelpiece and colourful paper bells hung at either end. Tucked behind every picture top was a sprig of holly.

Freddie sat down. "What's more it's a recreation of what it would have been like. Because having seen a couple of old Christmas photos in the Bray's family album of this room taken in the early nineteen-sixties, we were able to establish where the decorations went back then and we've put each in the same place."

Amelia chuckled. "It's a bit like being in a museum. You know, like when you visit a house that someone of note lived in and things are as they would have been during their residency."

"That's just what we've tried to create. A sense of yesteryear in the Bray household."

As Dilly sat down they heard the clonk of the letterbox. "Junk mail, I suppose," she grumbled, "that's all we ever seem to get. Although in the weeks before Christmas we received a lovely lot of cards from locals welcoming us to the village."

Dilly, in no rush to see what the postman had brought, finished her coffee and mince pie before she went into the hallway to collect the post.

"Oh dear. It looks like someone doesn't know Bert has died." In her hand she held a yellowing envelope addressed to Mr Albert Bray. "I should imagine it's a Christmas card." She laid it down on the table.

"Aren't you going to open it?" Amelia was curious to know who had posted it too late to arrive on time and who wasn't aware that Bert had died.

"It doesn't seem right," said Dilly.

Amelia laughed. "Well Bert won't mind, will he?"

"No, I suppose not," Dilly picked up the envelope and opened it. Her jaw dropped. "No way. It can't be, not after all these years."

Freddie frowned. "What can't be? Who's it from?"

She passed him the Christmas card.

"Good heavens, it's from Anthony." Freddie looked at the postmark on the envelope. "It's stamped Plymouth."

"What does it say?" Ernie asked.

"Not a great deal. Just, *Hello Bert. Hope you, Auntie Ethel and Uncle Frank are all well. I'm hoping to pop down to Cornwall when I have a few days off work at Easter. I'll stay in the pub and perhaps we can meet up for a drink. I won't come to the house for obvious reasons. With best wishes to you all for Christmas and the New Year, Your Cousin Anthony.*"

"No, but that's ridiculous," gasped Dilly, "I mean it's forty-seven years or whatever since Ethel and Frank died.

So even if this is the first time he's been in touch, common sense must tell him they've long since gone because they'd be well over a hundred if still alive."

"Absolutely," agreed Amelia, "What's more he can't still be working either. He'd have to be in his eighties now, so goodness only knows what he means by time off work."

"You're right he would be in his eighties. Perhaps his memory is playing tricks on him," reasoned Dilly, "you know, he's wandered into the past or something like that. Sadly it appears to be quite a common occurrence."

"Must be the case. Having said that, Bert said he never saw him again so he wouldn't know Frank and Ethel were dead for sure, would he?" Freddie looked again at the envelope. "No! I don't believe it. Here's the reason they lost touch. Look. The postmark says December 22nd 1975."

"1975! No wonder the envelope looks yellow," chuckled Ernie."

Dilly took the envelope from Freddie. "So are we to believe it's been lost in the post all these years?"

"Well, these things do happen," agreed Amelia.

"I can't see any other explanation," said Freddie, "and I suppose because Bert never received it and so never replied, Anthony wouldn't have come down the following Easter."

"He might have. We just don't know," Amelia picked up the card and read the message. "But whatever, it looks then as though we can rule Anthony out as a hit and run suspect because when he wrote this he clearly didn't know that Frank was dead."

"Nor Ethel," Freddie added.

"Unless he's pretending he doesn't know to make him appear innocent," reasoned Ernie.

"It's possible," agreed Dilly, "but as regards to whether or not he came down for Easter I think we can safely say he didn't. Remember, Bert said in his letter he never saw him again and that's why he bricked up his bike. Poor Bert thought it might have been used to run his dad down."

"But Bert's letter was written in January 1976 and so well before Easter," Amelia reminded them.

"Good point," said Freddie, "because had Anthony come down then and they'd met up, Bert would surely have unbricked his bike afterwards and destroyed the letter."

"So what are we to make of it?" Dilly asked, "Is Anthony innocent or guilty?"

"Well, with the Ouija board's reference to Popeye and with Anthony having been a sailor, my money's on guilty," Ernie was adamant.

"But how do we find out?" said Amelia, in exasperation, "There's no address on the card and a Plymouth postmark's not much help. Especially with it being forty-seven years out of date."

"We don't even know if he's still alive." In need of another coffee, Freddie stood, collected mugs and asked if anyone else wanted a refill.

As he left the room, Dilly placed the card on the mantelpiece beside the nativity scene. "So really this turning up today tells us absolutely nothing at all and we're right back to square one."

Chapter Eighteen

On New Year's Eve, Freddie went to the pub to meet up with Max, Dotty and Gerry. He tried to get Dilly to join them, but when Amelia mentioned it was usually very busy and noisy, she decided to give it a miss and instead spend the evening with Amelia and Ernie playing Scrabble at Yew Tree Cottage. As the clock neared twelve, Ernie turned on the radio and when Big Ben struck midnight they went outside to watch fireworks lighting up the night sky above the Duck and Parrot.

The following morning, Orville King, out for a walk to clear his muzzy head, called in at Lavender Cottage to see Bert's motorbike having been reminded about it by Freddie in the pub the previous evening. After viewing the bike and chatting with Ernie about it for a good half hour they returned indoors where Dilly insisted Orville join Freddie, her neighbours and herself for pre-arranged coffee to which he readily agreed.

"Is that Ethel's piano?" Orville asked as he took in his surroundings.

"Yes, it is."

"Well I never." He lifted the lid. "Do you play, Dilly?"

"I can play a bit but haven't done so simply because it badly needs tuning."

Orville ran his fingers across the keys. "Ouch, yes it does and I'd be happy to do it for you."

"Would you? Can you? I mean, if you could that would be wonderful."

He winked. "It's one of my many talents and as there's no time like the present, I'll do it now, if that's alright with you."

"Yes, that's fine. I'm not planning to go anywhere."

"Good," He stood, "I'll just pop home for my tools and be back in a jiffy."

When he returned Dilly insisted he have a mug of coffee before he commenced work and Orville happily sat down by the Truburn.

"I watched the weather forecast this morning," he said, as Dilly handed him coffee and a mince pie, "and apparently there's a bad storm on its way sometime this week, so being near to the sea you'll need to batten down the hatches. What's more they've named it Albert. Which I must admit made me chuckle."

"Yes, and Albert coincides with spring tides too," said Ernie, "and according to the weather experts in the pub yesterday lunchtime it could well do a bit of damage."

"I saw something about that on the local news," said Dilly, "but I've no idea what spring tides are."

"It's quite straightforward," said Orville, "Spring tides are when a high tide and the sun, moon and earth are in a line and the gravitational force is strong. It happens twice a month. The line-up of the moon and sun bring in gravitational forces and cause the highest and lowest tides of the month."

"Clear as mud," Dilly liked to be honest.

"Gobbledy-gook," agreed Amelia.

"I think it sort of makes sense," said Freddie, "but which direction will the wind be coming from?"

"South southeast. Worst possible way for us." Orville took a bite of his mince pie.

"They'll need to do something about the boats on the slipway then," reasoned Amelia, "because surely they'll be very vulnerable there."

"They already have," said Orville, "The kayaks went the day before yesterday and so did the gigs. The rest will no doubt get moved pretty sharpish. They don't have to take them far though. Just over the road and round the back of the petrol station. I saw Sassy Sal in there the other day so Zippy is prepared. But then the fishing boats don't go out over the Christmas/New Year period so I expect he tucked it away before the festive season, just in case."

Amelia placed her empty mug on the table. "That reminds me. I keep meaning to ask if Sassy Sal is named after a real person or is just made up."

"A real person," said Orville, "Sal was John's big sister. She was a cheeky minx but sadly she died in the early fifties. Poor kid was only fourteen. I didn't know her that well because she was quite a bit older than me. It was all very sad though."

"Oh dear. So what was the cause of death?" Amelia asked.

"She was ill for some time but I don't know any more than that. People didn't talk to kids about death and illness back then like they do today."

Amelia agreed. "We all led more sheltered lives before the internet. Not sure whether that's a good or bad thing."

"A bit of both, I reckon," Dilly picked up the tin of mince pies and offered them around again. "Anyway, going back to Storm Albert, I must say it sounds very exciting and in a funny sort of way I'm looking forward to it."

Orville took a second mince pie. "Thanks Dilly, they're smashing. Just like my old mum used to make. As for the storm, well, I don't think you'll be disappointed and to be on the safe side I'd move anything that might blow around to somewhere safe. You know, garden furniture, watering cans, potted plants. That sort of thing. Oh, and trampolines too but I doubt you have one of those." He chuckled mischievously.

When refreshments were finished, Amelia and Ernie went home and Orville took up his tools and set to work tuning the piano. While he was working, Dilly did as he had suggested and moved anything light and likely to blow around into the lean-to shed.

When Orville finished, Dilly reached for her purse and asked how much she owed him. To her surprise he refused payment and said he was happy to have helped and perhaps they could play a duet together sometime. After he left, Freddie chuckled, "You have an admirer. Orville's face lights up whenever you speak to him."

To Dilly's surprise, she found she was flattered.

The next day, villagers were dismayed to hear on the news that Storm Albert had been up-graded from orange to red alert meaning there was a threat to life and it would likely cause damage to property.

Two days later as darkness fell, the wind speed slowly increased as the edge of the storm drew nearer and by the time Dilly and Freddie turned in for the night it was blowing gale force eight. From the sea facing window in her room, Dilly sat for a while, clutching her hot water bottle and watching the waves of the ebbing tide as they tumbled and frothed in the light from a streetlamp. Eventually, knowing there would be little more to see until the tide turned and the wind speed increased further, she removed her dressing gown and climbed into bed where the sheet and duvet were warmed by yet another hot water bottle.

The following morning, the wind raged at storm force ten and salt spray trickled down the front windows of the cottage obscuring the view. Eager to see the waves, Dilly attempted to open her window but the strength of the wind forced it back into her hands and not wishing it to be blown from its hinges she gave up the struggle.

Downstairs, Freddie was up, dressed and eager to get outside.

"I've checked the tide table," he said as Dilly entered the living room, "And high water is in twenty minutes, so time for a quick cup of tea then we must go out and see what's happening."

Wrapped in warm coats, hats, scarves and gloves, Amelia and Ernie were already out on the pavement when Dilly and Freddie stepped from their front door. To prevent her small frame from getting blown over, Freddie linked arms with his godmother.

"Wow! This is amazing," Dilly tightly gripped the green railing with her free hand to retain her balance.

"It certainly is. As you know we've been here for ten years," shouted Ernie, trying to make himself heard over the howling wind and thunderous crashing of waves, "but we've never seen it anywhere near as rough as this. Admittedly the sea comes up over the road from time to time but this is unprecedented."

A car drove slowly by and they automatically stepped back to avoid getting splashed as it passed through sea water gushing down the drains. Feeling chilled, Amelia pulled up the zip of her jacket as far as it would go. "Is it safe to look over the wall in between waves?"

"No way," said Ernie, firmly, "far too dangerous and there will be nothing to see except litter and debris swirling in the dirty water. Even between waves the sea will be half way up the steps."

Huddled together they watched as beneath a leaden sky the wind buffeted everything in its path and water splashed over the sea wall. Along the road, sheets of Perspex on the sides of the bus stop shelter, rattled continuously while its roof, battered by the wind and drenched by the enormous waves, appeared to be holding on by a wing and a prayer. Within minutes, the clothes of the spectators were wet from the continuous salt spray. Gulls, looking for food attempted to fly but were unable to get off the ground. And as they watched they heard an almighty crash and turned just in time to see the roof blow off a garage further down the road. As it crashed into someone's front garden, Ernie concerned for their safety suggested they return indoors for coffee for he was also eager to make sure Oscar was not distressed by the excessive noise. All agreed and just in time, for as they stepped over the threshold of Yew Tree Cottage, the heavens opened and hailstones the size of marbles fell from the gloomy sky where they bounced, rattled and clattered along the pavement, the road and the roofs of cars parked alongside the kerb.

"Phew, that was close," Dilly, last in wiped her feet on the doormat, removed her sodden woollen hat and closed the front door.

Inside the kitchen, Oscar made a fuss of Ernie while Amelia pulled off her gloves and warmed her hands by the fire. "My fingers are all dead. When they're back to life I'll put the kettle on."

"No hurry, it's just nice to be back in the warm." Having removed her outer garments, Dilly wiped salt spray from the lenses of her spectacles and Freddie placed his jacket on the back of a chair.

After the kettle boiled they all sat around the table eating chocolate cake, drinking coffee and discussing the weather.

"How do you fancy beachcombing tomorrow, Dilly?" Amelia waved her hand towards the window where rain lashed against the small glass panes, "There could be all sorts washed up after this lot."

"That sounds very exciting. So, yes, count me in."

"I'd love to join you for a forage," said Freddie, "but I have a ceiling to plaster tomorrow."

"Oh, that's a shame. How about you, Ernie. Will you come with us?"

"I would but I've a dental appointment in the morning. Not looking forward to it as I need a wretched filling."

Dilly licked her finger to pick up the last cake crumbs from her plate. "Just the two of us then. So what time shall we go?"

Amelia looked at her husband. "When's high tide, Ern?"

"Well it was at eight twenty this morning so it'll be roughly nine twenty tomorrow."

"Ideal. So if we go around half ten there will be a bit of beach to search and we can do the rest as the tide goes out further."

"Well, you be careful," warned Ernie, "there will be a huge ground swell tomorrow so watch your step and don't forget your mobiles."

Amelia put the kettle on to refill the empty coffee mugs. "Don't worry, we'll keep well away from the water's edge."

Dilly woke up bright and early the following morning and looked from her bedroom window. To her delight she saw the wind had dropped to little more than a breeze. The sea, however, was still rough and the cloudy sky was a patchwork of gunmetal grey, black and dirty yellow.

Downstairs, Freddie was busily making sandwiches for his lunchbox. He looked up as Dilly entered the living room. "You'll need your gumboots this morning and looking at the sky probably an umbrella too."

"We'll be fine. After all it's not far to run if we need to dash home."

Dilly made tea for them both and then Freddie left for work wishing them luck and saying he should be home around four.

At half past ten, Amelia called for Dilly. With her she had Oscar. "I thought I'd bring him with us so he's not home alone. He looked so excited when he saw me put my coat on and I just couldn't bear to leave him. He only had a short walk with Ernie this morning, you see, because Ernie was pushed for time due to the dental appointment. I hope you don't mind."

"Of course I don't mind. He might even unearth something interesting."

Wrapped in thick coats, scarves and wearing gloves, the two ladies left with Oscar on his lead. Both carried an assortment of bags and bin liners in which to collect not only things of interest but inevitable debris too. As they climbed down the steps and set foot on the shingle Amelia unfastened Oscar's lead and the dog ran off across the beach causing a pack of gulls to take flight and squawk in annoyance, their scavenging cut short by the unwelcome intrusion.

"Oh, to have that much energy," laughed Dilly, as Oscar reached the slipway.

"Wouldn't it be nice, but you strike me as someone with plenty of energy anyway. I couldn't go jogging like you do. I like walking though and sometimes speed walk just for the challenge."

Because Oscar had gone in the direction of the slipway the ladies went that way too, both carefully scouring the beach for anything washed up by the storm. However, to their dismay, their initial search found very little of interest. Just several pieces of driftwood, segments of fishing nets, a gorilla basket with both handles missing and a battered lifejacket. Everything else was rubbish not dissimilar to that left on beaches everywhere after busy days in the summer. But then as they approached the slipway, Amelia spotted a bottle bobbing on the waves. She pointed it out to Dilly. "What do you think? There could be a message in it, couldn't there? It'd be so exciting if there was."

"It would but I think it's highly unlikely."

"Well, there's only one way to find out," As Oscar made his way back along the beach, Amelia put down her bags on the sand and waded into the sea. She even managed to grab the bottle without water seeping over the top of her gumboots. However, as she waded back towards the shore she tripped on a hidden rock, lost her footing and with a mighty splash tumbled head-first into the waves but still clinging onto the bottle. Trying not to laugh lest she be hurt, Dilly stepped into the water and pulled Amelia to her feet. The bottle was green and had no doubt had once contained wine. But to Amelia's disappointment it now held nothing but salt water.

"Never mind," said Dilly, "I'm feeling quite chilly anyway so I suggest we call it a day and head back home to get you out of those wet things."

Reluctantly Amelia agreed.

Dilly cast her eyes along the beach in both directions. "Where's Oscar?"

"He won't be far away." Amelia called his name.

From the far end of the beach, Oscar emerged from a cave and hurtled across the wet sand with something in his mouth.

"Trust him to find a bone," laughed Amelia.

When Oscar dropped the bone at their feet Amelia bent down to pick it up in order to hurl it along the beach for Oscar to chase, but before she had a chance, Dilly stopped her.

"Let me see that." Amelia handed over the bone. "I may be wrong but I'm pretty sure this isn't from an animal. I think it's human. In fact I'm pretty sure it's this bone here." Dilly patted her arm.

"But where did he find it?"

As if he understood, Oscar snatched the bone from Dilly's hand and ran back across the beach. The two ladies followed and when they caught up with the dog, he led them into a cave. Dilly took her phone from her pocket and switched on the torchlight. Away from the entrance Oscar dropped the bone on a pile of cobbles and with tail wagging pawed away at the stones. Before they could stop him, another bone surfaced. Amelia grabbed Oscar's collar to prevent him disturbing the bones further. As she did so, Dilly instinctively rang the police.

"Who do you think this poor soul is?" Amelia asked as Dilly ended the call.

Feeling light-headed, Dilly lowered herself onto a large rock. "Goodness only knows. Probably before our time because these bones look pretty ancient. As she flashed her torchlight to take another look, she spotted something lying by her feet. She bent down, picked it up and placed it in the torchlight. "Whatever this is it's badly tarnished but looks like some sort of band."

"Might be a bangle. If so it could have fallen from the arm bone thing when Oscar picked it up."

"Sounds feasible." Dilly took a handkerchief from her pocket and gently rubbed the metal. When she saw an inscription, the colour drained from her face. "What on earth does this mean, Amelia? There's a name here and it's George Bray."

Chapter Nineteen

When the police arrived they sent Dilly and Amelia back to Yew Tree Cottage so that Amelia could change out of her wet clothes and it was agreed a police officer would join them in due course to take statements. While Dilly waited in the warm with Oscar for Amelia to shower and change, she mulled over their gruesome find and the consequences thereof. For she and Amelia had already agreed while they had awaited the arrival of the police that the remains could not be George Bray, for as far as they knew he was buried in the village graveyard along with his wife, Elizabeth nee Jago. As she wracked her brains as to who the mystery person might be, she suddenly recalled a comment made by Bert in the letter he had placed beneath the seat of the Harley Davidson. It referred to an item Bert had given to his cousin.

'I gave him the copper bracelet given to me by my grandfather George Bray shortly before he died. Granddad wore it to help relieve the pain of arthritis and his name was engraved on its inside. Anthony was delighted and slipped it on his wrist. After all George was his grandfather just as much as he was mine.'

"Are you alright, Dilly?" Amelia, having entered the room dressed in warm clothing and with a towel wrapped around her wet hair, was puzzled by the frown on her friend's face.

"It must be Anthony. The body we found must be Anthony. Bert gave him their grandfather, George Bray's copper bracelet. So it has to be him."

"Yes, I'd forgotten that so you could well be right," Amelia switched on the kettle and took two mugs from the cupboard, "I wonder if the police will accept the bracelet as being proof of identity though."

"I doubt it but they must have other ways of finding out."

Amelia spooned coffee granules into the mugs. "But if it is him, how did he end up dead in a cave?"

"I've no idea but he wouldn't have buried himself and so I can only assume someone murdered him and put him there."

Amelia placed the mugs of steaming coffee on the table, removed the towel from her head and then sat down. "But who and why?"

"I don't know, I really don't, but I shall move heaven and earth to find out."

Oscar suddenly stood up and with tail wagging looked towards the back door where within minutes Ernie entered the kitchen his face slightly lop-sided due to the anaesthetic.

Seeing his wife's wet hair he attempted to smile. "Don't tell me you fell in the sea. I told you to be careful."

"No I didn't. Well actually I did but that's another story anyway." After making him coffee, Ernie sat down and Amelia told of Oscar's discovery in the cave.

"Ah, that'll explain the two police cars parked further along the road. I did wonder."

"What's bothering us," said Dilly, "is if there's no form of identification on the body then it might be impossible to say one way or another if the person in question is/was Anthony. I mean, yes, we found the bracelet but that could have been dropped and washed into the cave at some point and doesn't mean he was wearing it."

"There is a way," said Ernie, glad to put his coffee mug down due to finding it difficult to drink with a half-numbed mouth, "and the answer is Ivy Richards."

"Ivy. How can she help?" Dilly was nonplussed.

"Simple. DNA. Ivy's great grandmother was Victoria Jago and she was the sister of Anthony's grandmother, Elizabeth. Bert's grandmother too of course. All they need to do is take a mouth swab or whatever from Ivy and then do whatever the procedure is on the remains that you two and Oscar found."

Amelia chuckled. "Good thinking, Ernie," she said with pride, "we'll pass that on to the police when they call in for our statements."

News of the discovery in the cave travelled around the village like wildfire and with it Dilly's surmise that the victim was Frank Bray's nephew, Anthony Hammond. Until the body's discovery, very few knew Frank had a nephew but it made sense when they heard that uncle and nephew had had words before Frank had gone to the pub in a huff hours before he was knocked down and fatally injured in the infamous hit and run. By the end of the day most had concluded that Anthony was unquestionably to blame for Frank's death but no-one could fathom out who might have buried him in the cave and why. Meanwhile, the police, grateful for the information regarding the family connection between Ivy Richards and Anthony Hammond, should he be the deceased, asked the lady in question for her co-operation. Her reply was that she would be delighted to oblige.

Freddie awoke the following morning to see icy patterns on the window panes in his room. He shivered as he slid out of bed and reached for his dressing gown and slippers. With arms folded in an attempt to prevent himself shivering, he opened the window and looked outside. A sharp frost had turned the landscape into a winter wonderland. Freddie quickly closed the window and dashed downstairs reminding himself to tread carefully on the frosty path as he made his way to the small building at the bottom of the garden. After returning back indoors, he topped up the coke in the Truburn and then went up to his room to get dressed. Glad to be warm at last he made himself a mug of tea and toasted bread on the heat from the hot coke using his godmother's homemade toasting fork.

Later in the morning after Freddie had gone to work and the early morning frost had disappeared with the rising temperature, Dilly went to the post office to buy a stamp and post a birthday card and letter to her erstwhile next door neighbour. Amelia was with her as the two ladies planned to go for a walk when the card was posted and mull over thoughts regarding the death of Anthony Hammond, on the assumption that it was his remains they had found in the cave.

"How's your father?" Amelia asked Emma, the postmistress after Emma had commiserated with the ladies over their grisly discovery.

"Not good I'm afraid. He's been very dithery lately and yesterday he tripped on the rug in the hall and hit his head on the corner of the telephone table. I took him to the doctors and they said he seems okay but to keep an eye on him. Trouble is I can't be in two places at once and although I have help in the shop I can't leave the post office counter. His next door neighbour said she'll keep popping in but I felt guilty. Steve would help if he could because he's trained for post office work but he's half way through installing a bathroom and so can't leave it half done."

"Oh dear," said Amelia, "Would you like us to call in? We're going out for a walk now and can quite easily go that way."

"It'd be no trouble," Dilly added, "and it'd be nice to see him again."

"If you would I'd be most grateful. I'll be there myself in an hour or so when I close for lunch."

"Say no more. We'll go straight there now." Dilly paid for her stamp and stuck it on the envelope of her card.

"Thank you so much, and so that he doesn't have to answer the door please go round the back where the door will be unlocked and let yourselves in."

"Will do and don't worry we'll stay until you arrive."

"Thank you."

Once outside Dilly posted the card and the ladies made their way to the Buttercup Field Estate.

"Poor old Cyril," said Amelia, "I hope he recovers because his mind still works well."

"I agree. It must be very frustrating when the spirit is willing but the flesh is weak."

On arriving at Daisy Bank they did as Emma requested and followed the garden path around the side of the house to the back where Amelia knocked on the door, opened it slightly and called out saying they had seen Emma and had come to see how he was.

"Come in," a weak voice replied, "I'm in the front room."

They found Cyril sitting by the fire listening to a CD of Trenwalloe Sands' male voice choir. He appeared much frailer than when they last had seen him on Christmas Eve. His hands shook and he seemed less alert but at least he knew who they were.

"You're the nice lady who lives at Yew Tree Cottage," he said to Amelia. He turned to Dilly, "and you live in Bert's old place."

Amelia sat down beside him. "That's right, and you gave us the plans to our house from back when you knocked the two into one. My husband was really thrilled to have them. It made his day."

"Yes, he told me that when we were in the pub on Christmas Eve. Nice do that."

Amelia was relieved to hear he remembered. "Yes, listening to the choir made it feel very Christmassy."

Cyril nodded. "They're a smashing bunch of fellas. I really miss singing with them."

"Yes, I'm sure you do."

"Would you like us to make you a drink?" Dilly had taken a seat on the opposite side of the fireplace.

"No thanks. I've had two this morning and so I'll be alright 'til lunchtime. You ladies are more than welcome to make something for yourselves though."

"No, no, we're fine aren't be, Amelia?"

"Yes. Too many cups means extra trips to the loo."

Cyril chuckled. "Yes, a bit of a nuisance when you can't move too fast."

"Even more so when you have to nip down the bottom of the garden as we do," said Dilly.

"Oh yes, I remember we had to do that before we did Yew Tree up." Cyril laid back his head and closed his eyes. "Bert used to play the trumpet."

"In the brass band, yes. We found his trumpet in the cottage." Dilly was surprised by his random comment.

"His dad wasn't very musical. Frank I mean. His mother was though. She played the piano. I often heard her in the summer when the back door was open and I were out tending my vegetables. Nice lady was Ethel."

"I wish I'd known her," said Dilly, "I wish I'd known all the Brays."

Amazing Grace began to play. Cyril sighed. "Ah, one of my favourites. I always liked singing this, it makes me sad though."

With eyes still closed he slowly nodded his head in time with the music unaware the back door had opened and Emma had quietly entered the room. "Oh, is he sleeping?" she whispered.

"No just resting his eyes while he listens to the music. Apparently this is one of his favourites." Amelia pointed to the CD player.

Emma sat down. "Good, he looks content."

"Ethel used to play this. She'd sing it too. Nice voice she had. Nice lady was Ethel. I used to grow spinach and I'd take her some. She loved it, you see," Cyril chuckled, "Frank hated it though and he used to call me Popeye."

"Popeye," Dilly looked at Amelia who sat static in shock.

A tear trickled down Cyril's wrinkled cheek. "You poor fella. I didn't mean to do it, mate. It were an accident. I'd never have hurt you. Honestly, Frank, it were an accident."

"What was an accident, Dad?"

Cyril jumped and his eyes flashed open. "Emma, I didn't know you were here."

"I've only just arrived. What do you mean by accident?"

"What?" Cyril looked at the three expectant faces. "Oh, oh, I was…I was thinking out loud, that's all. Take no notice of me."

"No, I won't," Emma raised her voice, "What was an accident, Dad?"

Cyril's eyes flashed with fear. "Frank. I was thinking about Frank and his death. The music reminded me, you see."

"And what about Frank's death? And why are you sorry? Were you there? Do you know what happened?"

Cyril hung his head as though in shame. "Oh dear, me and me mumblings. I've let the cat out the bag now, haven't I? And yes, I was there so I suppose I'll have to tell you even though it was a long time ago." His eyes looked pleading, "I really do hate to have to admit this, Emma, but it was me who knocked him down. Frank, that is and not a day has passed since then without me wishing I could have turned back the clock."

"What? But how? Why didn't you stop, Dad? Why didn't you stop?" Emma looked on the verge of tears.

"Because I'd been drinking, that's why. Just two bottles, that's all, but probably enough to put me over the limit so I couldn't take the risk."

"Was Mum with you?"

"No, of course not. She was out with her mates at a works get-together because one of them was leaving. You must remember that."

"Dad, it was in 1975. I wasn't even born."

"No, no, I suppose not."

"So where had you been drinking?" Emma sat down on the arm of the couch.

"At home and I was on my way back there from the off-licence. I was gonna watch a film on the telly see and while I waited for it to start I drank two bottles of beer that were in the fridge. I got the taste then and wanted more so I drove to the off-licence. I know I should have walked but the film was due to start soon and we had no video recorders and stuff back then so I took the car because it'd be quicker."

"And you knocked poor Frank Bray down on the way back. Really, Dad, how could you?"

"It was an accident, Em. As I drove along the road I could see him on the pavement and he was staggering all over the place. I was only doing about thirty mile per hour but just as I got level with him he stepped out into the road. I tried to swerve but knocked into him and sent him spinning. He fell backwards and hit his head on the kerb. It was dark but I got out to look and I could see in the light from the lamppost that there was blood everywhere and he wasn't moving. It was horrible and I was scared so I got back in the car and drove home. There was nothing I could have done for him and I didn't want to be breathalysed.

What's more, as I parked the car I realised that I might be able to buy the house if Frank were gone. Heartless, I know but that made me feel a bit better. You know, I thought perhaps fate had stepped in. I felt sure Bert would sell the house, you see, and the empty one next door too. Bert was much more reasonable than his dad and so that was another reason for me to say nothing. Because if I'd have confessed they could have said I'd done it on purpose. To get the houses, I mean. I might even have been charged with murder and locked up."

"Oh, Dad, Dad, you silly, silly old man."

"Did Carol never find out?" Amelia felt she should say something.

"No, no. She'd have been horrified. She liked old Frank," He started to sob, "Poor Ethel. It killed her, you know. The shock of losing her husband killed her and that I do feel really bad about."

"You have forty winks, Dad and I'll go and get your lunch," Emma stood, looked at Amelia and Dilly in desperation and indicated they follow her. "What should I do?" she asked, when they were in the kitchen out of earshot, "Should I report it?"

Dilly slowly shook her head. "I don't know what to say. It was such a long time ago and nothing will be achieved by the police knowing."

Amelia nodded her agreement. "And it was said at the time that Frank was drunk and in the road so the driver was not really to blame for the accident. The only crime was he didn't stop and get help."

"And," Dilly added, "it was reckoned Frank died instantly so nothing would have been gained by the paramedics getting there any sooner."

"But at the same time it seems wrong not to report it," said Amelia, "and I'm sure Cyril would get nothing more than reprimand for having fled the scene."

Emma opened a tin of soup and poured its contents into a jug. "I think I'll sleep on it and decide how to go about it in the morning. But I will report it otherwise the guilt will hang over my head for ever." She placed the jug in the microwave.

"That's probably the best option," said Amelia.

Dilly agreed. "And now despite thinking the contrary, I hope the body we found yesterday isn't Anthony Hammond because a positive identification will fuel the gossip accusing him of something we now know he had absolutely nothing to do with."

"Yes, I've heard the gossip. In fact it's the only subject anyone talked about in the post office this morning. Poor Anthony. If it's him I hope he gets justice."

"Does your dad know about the discovery?" Dilly asked, "The body we found, I mean."

"No, I thought it best not to tell him and I've asked his neighbour to keep mum too. I think it might upset him even more. Him being one of the few people that met Frank's nephew. Assuming it is him, that is. But as you say, I hope it isn't."

As Emma buttered a bread roll, the back door opened. It was the next door neighbour calling to see how Cyril was. Saying she had nothing on that afternoon she offered to stay with him. There was an old black and white film on at half past two and she knew from previous chats with Cyril that it was one of his favourites. Emma thanked her profusely and poured the warmed soup into a dish. After sitting her father at the table and giving him his lunch she left him in the capable hands of his neighbour and made her way back to the post office. Dilly and Amelia, knowing there was nothing more for them to do, left at the same time.

"Do you still want to go for a walk?" Dilly asked Amelia as they stood by the garden gate wondering which way to go.

"I'm easy but the tone of your voice and look on your face tells me that you'd rather go home because there's something on your mind."

"There is and it's something we need to discuss, so let's go back to Lavender Cottage for coffee and a bite to eat."

Chapter Twenty

Dilly and Amelia said very little as they made their way back to Lavender Cottage. It wasn't until they were inside with hot drinks, baked beans on toast and were warming their feet by the fire that Amelia asked the question that had been on her lips since they left the Buttercup Field Estate. "You think it's possible that Cyril killed Anthony, don't you?"

"If the remains we found are Anthony, yes, I do."

"And your theory is?"

"We know Anthony took out Bert's bike at some point. My theory is that when he got back here he left the bike and went off to catch the bus, the stop being just down the road. Obviously I don't know what time that would have been but if he finished cleaning the bike before he took it out, a couple of hours could easily have passed, depending of course how far he went on it. If he was at the bus stop when the accident happened he would have seen it all."

"Feasible although a lot of 'ifs'," agreed Amelia, "and Anthony having met Cyril earlier on, albeit briefly, could have recognised him and would no doubt have felt annoyed when he saw him drive off leaving Frank for dead."

"Precisely."

"And even though Anthony hadn't got on with Frank during their brief meeting, at the end of the day Frank was still his mother's brother and his uncle too."

"Exactly," said Dilly, "and blood is thicker than water."

"So what do you think happened next?"

Dilly thought as she watched a blue tit pecking at a seed ball dangling from a hook above the living room window causing it gently to tap against the glass pane. "I don't know but I suppose it's possible that Anthony, knowing where Cyril lived, went after him to confront him. If so he might have threatened to tell the police and that would have scared Cyril because as he said earlier, he didn't want to be breathalysed. So when Anthony ran off, say back towards the phone box which is near the bus stop, Cyril went after him. A scuffle broke out, Cyril overpowered Anthony. Knocked him out. Dragged him across the beach into the cave and buried him in a shallow grave and covered it with sand, cobbles and pebbles."

Amelia frowned. "He would have needed a spade to dig a hole in the sand."

"No problem. If Anthony was dead he'd have gone back home for one. We know he was into gardening and grew veg because he used to take spinach to Ethel, so he must have owned a spade or two."

"I like your theory and think it's feasible but wouldn't it have been a bit risky? I mean, by then Frank might have been found and there would have been police everywhere. Bert said in his letter the street was awash with blue lights."

Dilly shook her head. "Might have been the case but the police wouldn't have gone onto the beach, would they? If they were looking for a hit and run driver they'd be focusing on the roads and traffic."

"Okay, I'll go along with what you suggest. But what about the beer Cyril bought from the off licence. If Carol saw the, I assume, empty bottles, she might have guessed he'd been out and possibly around the time the accident had occurred. If so she would have asked questions."

"And to give himself an alibi he probably said he'd been to the off licence in case the police did a house to house thing. He could have claimed he walked there as it'd only take fifteen minutes or so and then the same for the walk back. No-one would know he was in a hurry because he didn't want to miss the beginning of a film."

"How about the car then?" Amelia asked, "I mean would it have been damaged on impact? If so, might Carol not have commented on that?"

"Good point but I suppose he could have cleaned it up. I mean, for all we know he might have been a poor driver and the car had all sorts of scrapes and scratches on it. Lots of cars were old bangers in the seventies. Especially in rural areas."

"True and it doesn't really matter anyway. Cyril has confessed so the why and wherefores are not important."

Dilly sighed deeply. "So how can we prove Anthony witnessed what happened?"

"We can't and that's the problem. No CCTV in the seventies or mobile phones and even if there was, any records would have long since been destroyed."

"No computers and no DNA testing either. It must have been a hell of a job to catch criminals back then."

"It must," chuckled Amelia, "One thing we can do though is to find out if there was any form of identification on the remains we found. At least then we would know for sure it is Anthony, not that I have much doubt. And the obvious person to ask is Dotty with her boyfriend being a police officer."

"Would Gerry be allowed to tell her that?"

"I don't see why not. Because it happened a long time ago the police probably think the chances are that the murderer is dead."

"What's more, I should imagine Gerry would probably tell Dotty what she wants to know just for a quiet life." As Dilly placed her empty coffee mug on the rug by her feet she caught a glimpse of Christmas cards stacked on the sideboard after being taken from the beams on twelfth night. She cursed. "Damn. We've forgotten something; the card from Anthony. He sent it in December 1975 so he couldn't have died the same night as Frank, could he? So bang goes my theory."

"You're right," Amelia groaned, "So perhaps Anthony's not the victim at all and someone found the bracelet after Anthony had dropped it at the bus stop or wherever and the person in question lost it on the beach at some time or other."

"No, hang on, it might still be Anthony because he could have come down at Easter in 1976 as he said he would. And if that's the case perhaps Bert was out working somewhere so there would have been no-one home. While here Anthony could have seen Cyril and confronted him. Threatened to blackmail him even. After which Cyril did away with him as we've already suggested without Bert even knowing his cousin had set foot in the village."

"Meaning," said Amelia, "that Anthony witnessed the hit and run but did nothing about it. He then went home and just before Christmas sent the card to make it look like he thought his uncle was still alive and kicking, but of course Bert never received it."

"Exactly."

"But surely if he had witnessed the hit and run he'd have reported it."

"Not if he was glad to see his uncle dead," reasoned Dilly. "He probably thought Cyril had done him a favour."

Amelia sighed deeply. "I don't know what to think."

"I'm inclined to agree." Dilly stood up and reached for the kettle on the Truburn, "Anyway, another coffee? All this chat is making me thirsty."

"Yes please."

"I wonder if we ought to pop along and see John and bring him up to date," said Amelia, as Dilly spooned coffee granules into the two mugs, "It'd be interesting to see what he thinks."

Dilly looked at the clock. "Or to save time we could ring him. In fact I'll do that right now." She handed Amelia her coffee and then picked up her mobile.

Dilly was on the phone for a good five minutes. When she ended the call, she smiled broadly. "John's fascinated and certainly thinks we ought to pursue the matter." She chuckled, "and for that reason he suggests we have another boozy night with the Ouija board."

"Oh yes, I'm up for that and I know Ernie will be too."

"Same here and I don't think Dotty will take much persuading."

"That's all of us then, so when does John suggest we meet?"

"He's leaving that up to us but he's free every evening this week."

"Would tonight be too early?"

"Probably not. It's not Freddie's choir practice night so he should be free. How about you and Ernie?"

"If Ernie has anything planned I'm sure he'll drop it but to make sure I'll nip home and ask him."

"Good, and while you're gone, I'll ring Dotty."

Ernie was very enthusiastic about another boozy night and said he'd look out different bottles of his homemade wine. To make sure it was alright with Freddie, Dilly rang him at work and he was equally enthusiastic. Dotty likewise said she couldn't wait; Gerry was working late again so she'd be on her own. She also suggested asking Max who said after the first Ouija night she wished she had been there too. Dilly thought asking Max was an excellent idea and so Dotty said she'd ring her. Suddenly realising they would be an odd number she asked Dotty to invite Helen as well. Ten minutes later Dotty rang back to say Max and her mother were thrilled at being asked and Helen was about to start making cocktail pasties for the occasion.

"We're going to need a glass with a big bottom," chuckled Amelia, "eight fingers will need quite a bit of room."

"I've a dumpy lightweight vase with a large base. We can use that."

Amelia and Ernie were the first to arrive for the Ouija board night and with him Ernie carried six bottles of parsnip wine. "I know it sounds a bit weird," he said, "but it's really very nice."

"And having drunk several glasses over the years I can vouch for that." Amelia placed a large jug containing homemade cheese straws on the table.

Next to arrive was Dotty carrying a chilled bottle of chardonnay and a frozen pizza. Dilly was amused to see the jogger/blogger had wisely chosen to wear flat shoes.

Max and Helen rolled up soon after; Helen clutching a tin containing eight cocktail pasties and a dozen homemade sausage rolls, and Max with a case of lager and a bottle of prosecco.

Last but not least was John with a bottle of merlot, a large bag of crisps, packets of peanuts and a tub of Bombay mix.

Dilly put the pizza in the oven and then on the top of the sideboard, more spacious because Freddie had taken the television set into the front room, she arranged the other food along with a quiche she had made. After placing a pile of serviettes beside a jug of cutlery she turned to their guests, "Well we won't starve. The pizza should be ready in fifteen minutes. There are plates on top of the cooker so whenever you're ready, please help yourselves."

Meanwhile, on top of the piano, Freddie and Ernie had arranged drink bottles and cans along with a selection of glasses.

"We won't die of thirst either," Ernie sat down at the table having poured himself a bumper glass of parsnip wine.

"Are we going to plunge straight into ghost hunting?" Max eyed the cheese straws but conscious of calories opted for a stick of celery instead.

"Well, I don't know about everyone else," said Freddie, "but I think it'd be best if we had a few drinks and nibbles first to relax us."

Everyone agreed.

"Are you able to tell us what the police make of the remains?" Amelia asked Dotty, "I mean, do they think it was Anthony we found?"

Dotty sat down at the table. "Well until they get the DNA results it's not possible to say but most are of the opinion that it was Anthony you found. I don't know what they'll do if the DNA's not a match though because there was no other form of identification on him other than a faded membership card for a nightclub in Plymouth."

"Plymouth," said Ernie, "Might well be him then because Anthony lived in Plymouth in the nineteen seventies, didn't he?"

"Yes, he did," Dilly poured herself a glass of parsnip wine and sat down. "I think we must give a bit of thought as to what questions to ask. I mean, we can't simply barge in and ask 'who killed Anthony Hammond', can we? That's assuming we get hold of someone." She took a sip of wine, "Hmm, this is rather good, Ernie, and doesn't taste of parsnips at all." She held up her glass, "Crystal clear too."

"I think I might give that a go," Freddie dropped his empty lager can into a box for recycling and filled a wine glass with Ernie's concoction, "Anyone else up for a glass?"

"Pour one for me please," said Max, "I don't want to miss out."

"Not for me," said Dotty, "I don't want a repeat performance of last time so I'm sticking to chardonnay."

"Nor me," said Helen, "I'm driving."

"Oh, go on, Mum. Have a glass or two. We can always get a taxi home."

"Alright, but just a small one, Freddie."

John opted to stick with merlot.

After several rounds of drinks and various nibbles had been consumed they made room on the table for the Ouija board. There was no need to make new cards because Dilly had kept the original ones. She handed out a few to each guest who spread them out on their section of table to form a circle. Once done, Dilly placed the upturned, lightweight vase in the centre of the cards. She then lit candles and turned out the main light.

"Why do I feel so anxious?" Helen asked.

Max squeezed her mother's hand. "If it's any consolation, I do too."

Dilly topped up her glass with parsnip wine. "That's why we all need a drink."

Freddie tutted as his godmother spilled a little wine on the tablecloth from her overfull glass. "Right, so are we going to do the same as before?"

"What did you do before?" Max's eyes darted around the room and thought how eerie it looked in candlelight.

"We took it in turns to ask a question by going round the table, clockwise."

"So who's going to get the ball rolling?" Dotty giggled.

"I will," Freddie placed his finger on the upturned vase and asked everyone else to do likewise. "Are you all ready?"

Seven heads nodded.

"Right," Freddie cleared his throat. "If there's anybody here with us from the spirit world tonight, please make your presence known."

Nothing happened and so Freddie repeated the question. Again nothing.

"You try," he said to Max.

"No, Freddie. Don't give up. Third time lucky."

"Okay," Freddie closed his eyes, his face contorted with concentration, "Once again I ask, is there anybody here, there or anywhere in the spirit world wishing to speak with us tonight?"

The glass moved a few inches and then stopped abruptly; simultaneously, all heard three muffled taps.

"What the…" Before Dilly could finish her sentence, three more taps followed.

"It's the door," laughed Freddie, "Someone's knocking on the door." He stood up and left the room to see who it was. To the surprise of all, when he returned, Ivy was with him.

"Hello, oh, what's going on here," Ivy's eyes darted from the table to the candles to the bottles of wine, "Are you having a séance?"

"No, no we're just asking the Ouija board a few questions to see if we can find out what happened to Anthony." Dilly spoke as though to do so was an everyday occurrence.

"Really!" A look of excitement flashed across Ivy's eyes, "Can I play?"

"Of course," said Freddie, "after all in a roundabout sort of way you're related to the Brays. I'll just nip upstairs and grab a chair for you because there are none left in the front room."

"Thank you and that reminds me. Half an hour ago I had a call from the police. They fast-tracked the DNA test thing and confirmed there is a match between me and the poor chap you found. So without doubt he is, was, or whatever, Anthony Hammond."

Dilly sighed. "That's sad, although I suppose we never thought it would be anyone other than him."

"True, but at least knowing will help us decide which questions to ask," said Ernie.

"It does," agreed Amelia, "and it makes this little gathering more poignant too, because I don't know about everyone else but I'm more determined than ever to find out what happened to the poor lad." Nodding heads endorsed Amelia's words.

"Oh, and before I forget. This is why I'm here." Now seated at the table on an extra chair, Ivy took a photograph from her handbag, "I've been to see my cousin in Liskeard today. I'd already told her on the phone about the goings-on here and she said to pop up and see her so we could have a proper natter. I've only just got back and came straight here as I thought you'd like to see this. It's a photo of Victoria Snell, nee Jago, my great grandmother who is of course Elizabeth Bray nee Jago's, sister."

Dilly leapt to her feet, took the picture of Elizabeth from the wall and placed it beside the photograph of Victoria. "They're very much alike, aren't they?" She sat back down, "I can see a likeness to you as well, Ivy."

"That's just what my cousin said. Her name's Poppy by the way and you'll never guess what. She's into reading tealeaves just like our great grandmother's sister, Elizabeth, and what's more, she's given me a lesson or two. She only took it up recently after remembering her mother, my Auntie Jo, told her about it years ago."

"Ouch," hissed Dotty, "Too many names is making my head ache."

Ivy patted Dotty's arm. "Don't worry, love. You don't need to remember any of them."

"No, but we'd like to know more about reading tealeaves." As Dilly returned the picture of Elizabeth to its nail on the wall, Ernie poured Ivy a bumper glass of parsnip wine.

"And I'll be happy to tell you, but not now," Ivy pointed to the upturned vase, "This looks far more exciting and I'd love to know what happened to young Anthony."

"You're quite right, so perhaps we can pick up where we left off." Dilly placed her finger on the vase and urged Freddie to recommence with his thus far unanswered request.

Freddie placed his finger on the vase and everyone else did likewise. But before he had a chance to speak they heard more knocking.

"Someone else at the door," said Dilly, "Who on earth can it be?"

"I'm nearest so I'll go and see." Amelia left the room and went into the hall. Seconds later she returned with Orville King who had sheets of A4 paper tucked beneath his arm.

"Oh, sorry to interrupt. Are you having a party?"

"Sort of," chuckled Dilly, "Care to join us?"

He winked at the evening's hostess. "I'd love to," A look of confusion crossed his face as he eyed the circle of cards and upturned vase but rather than ask questions he tried to fathom it out for himself.

Freddie jumped up. "I'll get you something to sit on," When he returned from upstairs with another chair, Orville held out the sheets of paper. "You left these at the rehearsal the other night, Freddie. That's why I'm here. To return them."

"Did I? Silly me. I'd have been looking for them for the next rehearsal, so thanks for that," Freddie placed the chair in a gap made between Ernie and Ivy.

"My pleasure," Orville sat down and looked again at the bits and pieces on the table. "I've tried to make out what's going on here but I'm none the wiser. So what are you up to?"

Ernie poured the newcomer a glass of parsnip wine while John explained the situation as briefly as possible.

"Cyril knocked down Frank!" exclaimed Orville, "I'd never have guessed it was him in a hundred years." Dazed, he downed the wine without thinking and Ernie poured him a refill.

"We had agreed not to let it go outside these four walls," said Dilly, "but Cyril's involvement is an important development. Having said that, please keep the news to yourselves until Emma has a chance to report it to the authorities."

"Mum's the word," said Ivy.

"And I'll keep my trap shut too." Orville nodded and sniffed at the same time, "I can smell lavender. Is it your perfume, Ivy?"

"No. My perfume is musk. A favourite of mine since I was a teenager."

Ernie groaned. "Not the lavender again. The same thing happened last time we did this, Orville, and we never did get to the bottom of it. Mind you, I couldn't smell it then and I can't smell it now."

"The more whimsical amongst us wanted to believe it was the presence of Bert's granny, Elizabeth. She was very fond of lavender and named this house," declared Dilly.

"Lavender helped with her tealeaf reading too," said Ivy, "but Poppy and me can't really see how it'd help. We are going to look into it anyway."

With his gaze fixed on Dilly, Orville began to sing. *"Lavender's blue, Dilly, Dilly, lavender's green..."*

"...Stop," said Dilly, hands raised, "that's so annoying because lavender's not blue or green, it's mauve."

"Or white," Amelia added.

"Well, I suppose the leaves are green," reasoned Dotty.

"Yes, the leaves are green," agreed Dilly, "but the song implies it's the flowers that are green."

John groaned. "Looks like we're going off on a tangent again, Ernie."

"It does. Women and their wafts of lavender."

"Don't blame the ladies," said Orville, "it was my fault."

"Hmm," John addressed Freddie, "are you ready to try again, young man?"

"I am, so fingers back on the vase everyone." All obeyed. "Okay, so here goes. Umm, spirit or spirits as the case might be, I know I've already asked but I ask again, is there one of you out there in the spirit world who'd like to converse with us tonight?"

As before there was no response.

"Humph. I've tried four times now and no luck so I must be out of favour. You try, Max."

Max chuckled. "I expect it's really because there's no-one there," She tried to look serious, "Is there a spirit here in this house tonight who wishes to communicate with us?"

The glass slowly moved across the table and stopped at the 'yes'.

"Yikes. I didn't expect that. Over to you Mum."

Helen's voice was little more than a whisper. "Spirit, spirit, who…who are you?"

The glass moved to the E and then the T, the H, the E and finally stopped at the L.

"Ethel," squeaked Amelia, "Are you Bert's mother then?"

The glass flew across the table to the 'yes'.

"Amelia, it's not your turn to ask a question," scolded Ernie.

"Sorry. I couldn't help it."

Ernie tutted. "My turn now." He licked his dry lips. "Ethel my love. We're sorry to disturb you, but do you know about the recently recovered remains over the road?"

The vase moved to 'yes'.

"Your turn, Orville," Ernie thought the choir master looked paler than usual.

"Goodness me. Okay, well, spirit, I mean, Ethel. Did you know the remains are of your nephew, Anthony?"

The glass answered 'yes'.

"This is crazy," squealed Ivy.

"It is and it's your turn now," chuckled Amelia.

"Really, oh no," Ivy tried to compose herself, "Ethel, it appears your nephew was um, murdered. Do you know who it was that took his life?"

Without hesitation the glass moved to 'yes'.

"Oh dear. I feel quite faint," Dilly's voice quivered. "Ethel, was it Cyril? Cyril Thomas who grew spinach and used to live next door?"

To her relief the glass moved to the 'no'.

Dotty was next. "Jolly good, Ethel! I'm glad it wasn't Cyril because he's a nice old boy but then if it wasn't him, who was it?"

The glass slowly moved to the O, the L, then the I, the V and the E. It paused before moving back to the O and then the Y and finally the L.

"Olive Oyl," Ernie almost fell off his chair laughing, "Someone's acting the fool."

Dotty frowned. "Who's Olive Oyl?"

"Popeye's girlfriend," said Amelia.

"I think Ethel's spirit's been on the parsnip wine," hiccupped Helen.

"I'm inclined to agree," Dilly turned to the historian, "Come on, John. See if you can get a sensible answer."

"Okay. Ethel, it's John here. John Martin. You must remember me albeit a long time ago since our paths crossed. My brother, Bruce, worked with Frank and Bert for a while. Anyway, I'll ask you the same question. Who killed Anthony?"

Without hesitation the glass moved towards the B.

"Not Bluto surely," chuckled Ernie.

"Shush," said Amelia, as the glass moved to the E. It then slid across the table to the R and finally the T.

"Bert," screamed Dotty, "No way."

As she screamed, the vase flew from the table, smashed against the wall and fell to the floor in a hundred tiny pieces. Everyone sat stunned.

"Put the light on, Freddie," Dilly was shivering.

"How did that happen?" Max asked, "The vase, I mean. How did it manage to fly across the room like that?"

"Probably more pressure on one side than the other so it shot off," reasoned Ernie, "A bit like when you play tiddly-winks."

"Tiddly-winks," chuckled Helen, "tiddly-winks wasn't like that last time I played."

"What's tiddly-winks?" Dotty asked.

"It's a game played with counters," said Dilly, "The aim is to flick one counter with another and get it into a beaker."

"Never mind the glass and tiddly-winks," said Amelia, "What about the name Ethel gave. I mean, surely she's not accusing her own son of murder."

Ernie nodded. "I agree. No mother would do that, surely. Especially when all concerned are dead and buried. What would be the point?"

"I can't give her a motive but I reckon it's more than feasible," reasoned John, "Ethel died a few days after Frank and so knowing Bert killed his cousin might have been a contributing factor of her death, along with losing her husband of course."

"But as far as we know Anthony wasn't killed on the same day as Frank's accident. Because of the Christmas card we have reason to believe he went back to Plymouth that night and didn't come down here again 'til the following Easter," said Freddie, "Meaning, Ethel would have died well before then."

Dilly frowned. "So what makes you think Anthony was killed around the same time as the hit and run, John? Although I must admit that Amelia and I initially thought that too, but because of the card we changed our minds."

"For the same reason, I suppose. After all earlier today we suspected Cyril of being involved because he had the means and a motive. As for the card, well, I'd just forgotten all about it."

Orville's eyes flashed from face to face as people spoke. "What's all this about a Christmas card?"

"I was just about to ask that," said Ivy.

Dilly, with help from everyone else, explained about the card's unexpected arrival in the post.

"I see," said Orville.

"You're sharper than me then," Ivy topped up her glass, "I'm completely confused."

John turned to face Dotty, "Have the police given any indication as to when Anthony died?"

Dotty shook her head. "No, and Gerry reckons it'll be impossible to be any closer than a two to three year span."

"So he could have died on that first visit in September 1975, or Easter 1976. If he came down then, of course. Not much help, is it?" John took a handful of peanuts from a dish on the sideboard.

"Having thought about it I'm pretty sure Anthony didn't come here at Easter in '76," said Dilly, "simply because the letter Bert left in his bike said he never saw his cousin again."

Amelia frowned. "He also said he never heard from him again but we know for a fact that Anthony sent Bert a Christmas card because we've seen it."

Ernie laughed. "But Bert didn't get the card, did he love? It only arrived the other day. Meaning he wouldn't have known Anthony intended to come down at Easter."

"Of course. Silly me. We were here when it arrived."

"Well if you ask me," said Freddie, "I reckon Anthony didn't come down for Easter because if he had Bert would have dug out the bike and destroyed the letter saying he suspected his cousin of the hit and run."

The colour drained from Amelia's face. "Unless, as the Ouija board said, Bert killed his cousin and left the letter to give himself a posthumous alibi, should Anthony's remains ever be found."

"But what could be his motive?" Max asked.

Amelia shook her head. "Goodness only knows."

"Are we going to tell the police what Ethel said?" Helen found it hard to keep a straight face.

"Not unless we want to get sent to the funny farm," Ernie opened the last bottle of parsnip wine.

"But we don't know for sure that it was Ethel," reasoned Ivy, "I mean, it could well have been an imposter in the spirit world who was feeling impish."

Dotty walked over to the piano and filled her glass with chardonnay. "Well, whatever, there's no need to bother the police. When I see Gerry tomorrow I'll tell him what happened tonight. Then it's up to him whether or not he passes on to his colleagues what the impish spirit or Ethel had to say."

Chapter Twenty-One

Dilly woke just before six the following morning and was instantly wide awake. Knowing she was unlikely to get back to sleep, she slipped out of bed, dressed and crept downstairs hoping not to disturb Freddie who she could hear quietly snoring in the end room. After nipping down the garden path with a bucket of water, she returned to the house, tipped coke onto the glowing cinders in the Truburn and then made herself a mug of tea. As she warmed her hands on the mug her thoughts returned to the previous evening. Something wasn't right and she didn't believe for one moment that Bert was responsible for his cousin's death. Furthermore, she didn't believe they had made contact with Ethel which meant someone had been controlling the vase. But who and why, and why incriminate Bert? Was he or she trying to throw everyone off course to protect the real killer, or were they simply acting the fool? Dilly pondered over who might be trying to protect someone. It certainly wasn't herself. Nor Freddie as he was new to the area. Likewise so was Dotty and she wasn't even born when Frank and Anthony died and neither was Max. Helen was a native and could have been trying to protect someone but she wasn't at the first Ouija board night and it seemed highly unlikely that she was in any way involved. She didn't think for a minute Amelia and Ernie were culpable either because they had been in the village for only ten years. What's more, they liked Bert and so would never have poured scorn on his name. She thought about Ivy. Ivy had known Bert and was a distant relative and so it was unlikely she would incriminate him. Could she be protecting her late father? Possibly but there wasn't a jot of evidence to suggest a link between him and Anthony. Then there was Orville. She knew very little about him but he seemed a good sort and there was no obvious link between him and Anthony either. The only other person was John. Thinking of him reminded her that John, like Amelia and herself, had initially forgotten about the Christmas card mentioning Anthony's intended visit to Cornwall at Easter. Dilly put down her empty mug and went to the drawer where the card from Anthony was kept. She took it from its envelope and laid both down on the table. It was then that she noticed the writing inside the card was different from the writing on the envelope. Furthermore, the envelope was written in black ink, most likely a fountain pen, whereas the card was written in blue ballpoint. She scratched her head. Did this mean then that the card was not sent by Anthony at Christmas 1975 and been lost in the post, but was actually sent to distract them or to protect someone? But protect who? Cyril was their only real suspect to date. She sat down to think further. Could Cyril be the murderer? Ethel via the Ouija board said not but they knew he was responsible for the death of Frank and the fact they suspected him was the reason for the Ouija board get-together. But if it had been Cyril, why would someone turn suspicions to Bert? And once again, who? As she wracked her brains trying to make sense of it all, she heard footsteps on the stairs and then Freddie entered the room.

"You're up early," he yawned.

"I was just about to say the same to you, Freddie," Dilly stood up, "cup of tea?"

"Yes please, after I've been for a trip down the garden path."

When Dilly heard Freddie in the kitchen washing his hands she made him tea and another mug for herself.

"Why's Anthony's Christmas card out?" he asked, after seeing it on the table.

"I was thinking about last night and wanted to read what it said again and when I did I spotted something I'd not noticed before. See if you can spot it too."

Freddie picked up the card, opened it, read the message, looked at the back and then looked at the front. He did the same with the envelope and then slipped the card inside it. "I can't see what you mean unless it's that the envelope isn't the one made for the card because it's slightly too big."

Dilly took the card and envelope to see for herself. "You're right. I hadn't noticed that."

"So what was it you wanted me to spot then?"

"The writing on the envelope is different to the writing in the card. Two different pens have been used too."

Freddie frowned. "So what does this mean?"

"I'm not sure but I've a feeling the card wasn't sent by Anthony but by someone trying to throw us off track."

"Okay, but what about the 1975 postmark?"

"Yes, I know. That's the bit that's baffling me."

Freddie picked up his mug of tea and sat down. "Would Cyril have been able to drum up a fake envelope? I mean, he was a suspect yesterday and he was also postmaster for several years."

"True, but he's not postmaster now and the card only arrived the other day."

"Could Emma be involved?"

"I don't think so. She was genuinely shocked when she realised her dad was responsible for Frank's death."

"In that case someone must have had an old envelope dated December 1975 and addressed to Bert and they've used that." Freddie waved his hand towards the drawers in the sideboard. "We may even have a few here ourselves."

"I don't doubt we have but why would anyone else?"

Freddie sighed. "Goodness only knows."

Dilly sat up straight. "It has to be Cyril. Living next door he'd have known the family for years and so one of them could easily have used an old envelope to pass something on to him. Seeds for example, and for some reason he still had it."

"Would have to be Bert that gave it to him then because by December 1975 Ethel and Frank had both died."

Dilly sighed. "That's true."

"So you think that someone sent the card to throw us off the track because that someone has something to hide?"

"Yes, and I've just thought of something else. The card was delivered on Boxing Day. Boxing Day is a Bank Holiday so there would have been no post. We've been conned, Freddie, but if we can find out who sent the card, we'll have our killer."

Like Dilly and Freddie, Dotty was also trying to make sense of the events from the previous evening. So when Gerry called round as she finished her breakfast she was glad to tell him just what had happened. To her delight he seemed genuinely interested but confessed he couldn't really expect his colleagues to act on the ridiculous notion of the spirit of a long deceased member of the Bray family naming the murderer of Anthony Hammond. Especially when said informant was the mother of the accused. To use his own words, he said the whole thing was bonkers. Dotty, however, was not one to give up and so as Gerry had the day off work she suggested they go and visit Marge and Maurice Freeman, Gerry's parents, to see what they thought. For she knew that, not only were they living in the village when the hit and run had taken place, but that Maurice, a retired police sergeant, was on duty that night and was one of the officers who had attended the scene.

Marge and Maurice lived along the main street at the opposite end of the village to Lavender Cottage. Their three storey house was a large semi-detached with magnificent sea views and during the summer season they offered paying guests use of their three spare bedrooms to boost their pensions.

Over cups of tea, Dotty reiterated the events of the second Ouija board night leaving out nothing so that Gerry's parents were able to visualise the full picture. She did, however, ask that they keep Cyril's involvement to themselves until Emma had reported it.

"I've heard about Ernie's homemade wines," said Marge, "but I can't remember who it was talking about them now. Anyway, whoever it was said they were going to give it a go and start with rhubarb."

Maurice tutted. "Goodness knows what Ethel must have thought of you all throwing vases at the wall and boozing in her house. She was very house-proud and tee-total too although to be fair she didn't mind others drinking, just didn't like the stuff herself."

"But it looks as though the vase breaking was an accident," reasoned Marge, "and not the result of unruly behaviour."

"True," laughed Gerry, "on the other hand, it might have been broken deliberately by Ethel herself to show her disapproval of the goings on."

"Ah! So do you all think Ethel was there then?" Dotty was thrilled by the comments from Maurice and Gerry.

"I didn't say that," Maurice chuckled, "although I suppose I did imply it."

"I was only teasing. Seriously though, does what we did last night help in any way?"

Maurice shook his head. "Not really. It was a long time ago and despite what you say, I can't see as either Bert or

Cyril would have had the bottle to murder young Anthony. Certainly, Bert was a tearaway when in his late teens but he'd quietened down by then and kept himself to himself. As for Cyril, well Cyril always struck me as being a gent and I must confess, I'm saddened to hear he was involved in the hit and run."

"Me too," agreed Marge, "but as regards Bert, they do say the quiet ones are always the worst."

As Dotty was about to respond her phone rang. She pulled it from the pocket of her jeans and saw the caller was Dilly. "Ah, now this might be interesting," She stood up, "It's Dilly. Excuse me while I pop out into the hall to take it and not disturb you while I see what she has to say."

Three minutes later she returned with a huge grin on her face and explained Dilly and Freddie's observation of the Christmas card and its envelope.

Maurice wagged his finger. "Ah, now I can help you there because that's what the Brays did. Use old envelopes, that is. It was Frank who started it. He got Ethel to save them all, especially ones from Christmas cards, and then he'd use them to put in quotes and bills too, no doubt. He'd then drop them off by hand. He never even bothered to cross out his name and address since he delivered them himself. He believed in the old adage, you see, that if you take care of the pennies the pounds take care of themselves. Which I suppose was quite sensible really because there was no recycling back then. Not like today anyway."

"So are you suggesting that someone wrote a Christmas card pretending to be Anthony," said Marge, "and then stuck it in an old envelope already addressed to Bert and pushed it through the letterbox at Lavender Cottage?"

Dotty nodded. "Well yes, and it makes sense because it gives the illusion that Anthony came back to the village at Easter in 1976."

"But we know he didn't," said Gerry, "because he was already dead."

Dotty frowned. "But I thought you were unable to be sure of the year of his death. That's what you told me anyway."

"You're right, I did, but now they've established the remains are definitely Anthony, they've further examined his clothing. Well, what was left of them, and in the lining of his jacket they found a scrap of paper. Intense examination has revealed it to be a bus ticket. They can just about make out the date and it's September 1st 1975."

Dotty gasped. "Which according to Bert's letter is when Anthony first appeared on the scene. The day Frank was killed in the hit and run."

"Interesting," mused Maurice, "because in my opinion that means whoever wrote the Christmas card is either the murderer or is covering up for someone else who is or was, as the case might be. What I'm trying to say is, there's a chance that the person in question could well be dead after all this time."

"If you were to get hold of the card, could you get a handwriting expert to look at it?" Marge asked, "You know, to do a character analysis. It might narrow it down a bit."

"I suppose so," said Gerry, "they're very good at character analysis and handwriting comparisons although without the writing of suspects there's nothing to compare it with."

"Bert and Cyril are possible suspects," said Dotty.

"Yes, but Bert's dead, so he didn't write the card and I think Cyril's far too doddery now to have walked round the village and sneakily posted it through a letterbox in broad daylight."

Chapter Twenty-Two

John Martin sat at the table in his dimly lit kitchen drinking coffee and watching birds feeding on nuts, seeds and apple on the bird table in his small courtyard. His head ached a little, for although he liked a drop of wine most nights he was not accustomed to drinking a whole bottle as he had done the previous evening. His one consolation was that the wine he consumed had been merlot and not Ernie's parsnip.

John chuckled as he recalled the Ouija board and the looks of horror on the faces around the table after he had spelled out Bert's name with the up-turned vase. Not that he'd intended to use Bert's name. His plan was to spell out Bluto but Ernie was too quick and so having already gone to the B the only name that came into his head was Bert. Good choice though but he wished he'd been able to capture it on his phone. But with only one free hand it wasn't possible and it would have been a bit of a giveaway as to his guilt had he done so. He looked down at his elderly black Labrador. "Shame though isn't it, Ben, because it would have raised a titter if I could have put it on Facebook, especially the bit where the women screamed as the vase did its flying act. Pity it broke though. Perhaps I ought to buy Dilly a new one."

He finished his coffee and then reached for his jacket and Ben's lead, both hanging on the back of the door. "Time for walkies, I think. See if I can clear my head a bit."

Inside Yew Tree Cottage, Amelia was busy making breakfast for herself and Ernie. She had a slight headache but her husband on rising had insisted he felt fine. Just as the breakfast was ready, Ernie came in from outside, a bucket in his hands.

"Well timed," Amelia placed two plates of grilled bacon, poached eggs and grilled tomatoes on the table and then sat down. "What's in the bucket?"

"Parsnips," Ernie placed the bucket by the sink, washed his hands and took his place at the table, "Thanks, love. Just what I need. It's bloomin' cold out there."

"Yes, it looks it. So are you planning to make more wine?"

"I certainly am. Ouija nights have given the stocks a bit of a bashing. There's only three bottles of parsnip left from two years ago now so we'll have to start on last year's soon. Mind you, I still have plenty of gorse, rhubarb, rice & raisin, and apple so we won't go without."

"Thank goodness for that."

"Poor Helen, I should imagine she's not feeling too good this morning. She drank a fair bit for someone who doesn't indulge very often." Ernie chuckled, "She showed great interest in wine making early in the evening before we started the Ouija stuff and I told her to give it a go and start with dandelion. Out in the country she'll have all sorts of goodies on her doorstep. It'd be a doddle."

Before Amelia could answer, the phone rang. It was Dilly eager to share the thoughts of Freddie and herself regarding Anthony's Christmas card.

When Max entered the farmhouse, having taken out one of the horses for a run, she found her mother curled up in an armchair by the Cornish Range in the kitchen.

"Oh dear, Mum, do you feel as bad as you look?"

"Probably worse. How about you?"

"I'm fine. Cup of tea?" Max reached for the kettle gently boiling on the stove.

"Yes, please and a couple of aspirin if you'd be so kind."

When tea was made and aspirins distributed, Max sat down opposite her mother.

"I was thinking about last night while you were out riding," said Helen, "and I'm not sure what to make of it. Mind you, there are bits I can't even remember. Like getting home for instance."

"We left just before midnight and came home in a taxi. I offered to help put you to bed but you insisted you were fine."

Helen groaned. "Ugh, famous last words."

"You left your handbag behind too. Freddie sent me a text this morning and said he'd drop it in later. I said not to worry because we'd have to drive over sometime to pick up your car but he insisted saying he'd like to get out for a while and the fresh air up here would help clear his head."

"That's very sweet of him."

"It is. Anyway, back to last night because I was thinking about it too while I was out riding and I don't know what to make of the Olive Oyl reference. I mean, that was daft, wasn't it? What's more there's no way anyone will convince me it was Bert's mother we were communicating with."

"I have to agree," said Helen, "although it seemed perfectly reasonable last night. I'll blame the wine for that. I dread to think how much I drank but I was so swept up with the magic of it all, at the time I didn't care. Having said that, I rather like the idea of making wine, especially flowery ones. Ernie told me that dandelion is good to start with. It's nice and light, so I might give it a go."

Max laughed. "Good for you and I'm pleased to see you're not letting a silly headache put you off a possible hobby."

Helen took a sip of tea and leaned back in her chair. "What did you make of the Ouija board naming Bert as Anthony's killer?"

"I think it's nonsense and someone was being silly. But then I would think that, wouldn't I? I mean, were Great Aunt Mary to have married Bert, he'd have been my great uncle so I can't possibly think of him as guilty of any wrong-doing, especially murder."

"Oh dear, I hadn't thought of that. I do hope Mary wasn't around to hear what was said."

"Listen to you, Mother," laughed Max, "No-one was there. At least not from the spirit world."

"No, I suppose not. I hope last night shed a bit of light on something but I doubt it. I mean, other than Bert's name cropping up everything else was insignificant."

"I agree and I think the answer lies elsewhere. That Christmas card for instance. The one allegedly from Anthony. Something about that doesn't ring true but I'm not sure why I think that."

Inside her bungalow behind Chapel Terrace, Ivy sipped lavender tea from a bone china cup, part of a set given to her parents on their wedding day back in 1930. As she drank to the soothing sound of Chopin, she concentrated her thoughts on Anthony Hammond.

The tea was not at all to Ivy's liking but she was determined to drink it in order to read the tealeaves when she had finished. For Ivy, after the events the previous night, was as keen as anyone to learn just what happened to Bert's young cousin.

When the teacup was nearly empty, Ivy swirled the remaining liquid in a clockwise direction, three times. She then drank what was left and placed the cup on its saucer. But before she continued, she went to the fridge and poured herself a glass of grapefruit juice to take away the bitter taste in her mouth. She then lit two lavender scented candles, hoping the magical perfume would enhance her, albeit dubious talents, in the art of tasseology.

John had chosen the beach for his walk with Ben so that he'd be able to sit for a while on a boulder while Ben jumped in and out of the waves. The morning was fine and the sea relatively calm, however it was chilly and so after a while he called Ben to his side and the two made their way home. As they reached the front door John's mobile phone rang. It was Dilly telling him of their thoughts as regards the Christmas card from Anthony and the possibility of it being from someone else. John agreed it was an interesting theory and said as he'd nothing else planned he'd pop round to see her. When she ended the call she told Freddie what John had said.

"Ideal, and while you're chatting I'll drive over to Hilltop Farm with Helen's bag."

Freddie was just leaving when John arrived. The two men exchanged a few words as Freddie made his way to his van, having told John not to bother knocking but to go straight in as his godmother was eagerly awaiting his arrival.

Inside Lavender Cottage, Dilly showed John the difference between the writing on the card and that on the envelope and he agreed it was unlikely they were written by the same person.

"So how do you propose to establish who might have written the card?" John asked, as he removed his coat, "assuming it's not from Anthony, that is."

"I'm not sure but my gut instinct tells me it must be from someone local with something to hide and so most likely someone in the village."

John chuckled. "Well, you can hardly go round the village asking everyone for a sample of their handwriting."

"I agree. There must be another way though." Dilly glanced around the room as though looking for inspiration and in doing so saw the stack of Christmas cards on the sideboard by the television. "Of course. Why didn't I think of that before?" She picked up the cards and placed them on the table. "Several of these are from friends and relatives up-country but we also had quite a few from locals welcoming us to the village which we thought was really nice. It'll most likely be unproductive but why don't we go through them and see if we can see a likeness between the writing on any of these and the one allegedly written by Anthony Hammond?" She then opened up Anthony's card and stood it at the side of the table so both could see the writing to make comparisons.

"Yeah, why not? But before we go through them be a sweetheart and make me a coffee. I usually have one when I get in after walking the hound but today, because of your call, I came straight round here instead and I'm still feeling a bit dehydrated after last night."

"Good idea. I could do one myself anyway for the very same reason." Dilly stood up and took two mugs from the kitchen cabinet, "I'll cut a couple of slices of fruit loaf too. I'm sure you must be peckish after your walk."

"Lovely, thank you and while you're doing all that I'll put these cards into two equal piles so we each have the same amount to go through."

When coffee was made and fruit loaf buttered, Dilly placed plates and mugs on the table. She then went to sit down opposite John. As she walked around the table she noticed something peeping from beneath the cushion on his chair. Thinking it looked like a piece of card she made no comment, but quickly averted her eyes and sat down.

John took a sip of the coffee. "Hmm, lovely. Just what the doctor ordered."

Dilly smiled sweetly. "Good. I'll make a start on my pile now then." She took a bite of fruit loaf and hoped John didn't notice her hands were shaking.

Ten minutes later, John closed the last card on his pile and leaned back in his chair. "Nothing here anything like. How about you?"

"Same with me," Dilly drank the last of her coffee, "Shall we swap piles just to make sure neither of us missed anything?"

"Yes, why not?" John pushed his cards across the table to Dilly and she pushed hers towards him. Trying not to look too eager, Dilly went through her cards not looking for styles of writing, but for one card in particular. As she feared, it wasn't there.

"You went through them quickly," laughed John.

Dilly could feel her heart thumping. "That's because the one I was looking for isn't here and it's not amongst the ones you have either."

John frowned, the tone of her voice had clearly unnerved him. "What do you mean? What were you looking for?"

"The one I suspect you're sitting on. The one from you."

Chapter Twenty-Three

With a face like thunder, John leapt from his chair; as it toppled over and banged into the sideboard, the Christmas card he'd hidden beneath the cushion dropped onto the floor. With arms outstretched he dashed round the table and grabbed Dilly by the collar of her blouse. "How very clever of you, Ms Granger," he hissed, "You're pretty smart for a PE teacher."

Dilly tried to respond but the grip on her garment was too tight. Fearing the worst she glanced around the room looking for something, anything, to hit him with. As she realised there was nothing, a miracle happened. The bunch of lavender she had hung on the beam fell from its hook and tangled itself in John's hair. Distracted, but not wanting to loosen his grip, he shook his head hoping to dislodge what he fearing to be a huge spider. As the bunch of lavender dropped onto the floor, the back door opened.

"Coo-ee, it's only me. Ernie's taken Oscar out so I thought I'd come for a natter about the Christmas card."

The back door closed and then the door in from the kitchen opened. "What the…"

While John was preoccupied with his next move, Dilly took action. With a flip of her arm and a kick of her leg she threw John onto the floor and quickly knelt on his chest. "Hello, Amelia. You've arrived just in time."

Amelia stood her mouth gaping open. "But why, what…?"

"Look down there on the floor," Dilly nodded towards the card lying face down.

Amelia picked it up. "It's from John. I remember you showing it to me when it arrived. You said how much you liked glittery snow scenes. We had one similar, no doubt from the same pack."

"You're quite right, but now compare the writing inside it with Anthony's card standing on the table."

Amelia picked up the card and gasped. "Oh my goodness, the writing is identical." She looked at John, her face a picture of confusion, "So if it was you, why ever did you do it? For a joke? To throw us off course? I'd love to know."

"So would I. And when he's got his breath back he'll explain, won't you, John?"

John looked dazed. "How did you do that?"

"How did I do what?"

"Knock me over, fling me through the air or whatever you did."

"Oh that. Didn't I ever mention to you that I'm a black-belt in judo? Not bad for a PE teacher, eh?" She mockingly patted his flushed cheek, "I hope I haven't broken any bones."

Feeling her legs turn to jelly, Amelia sat down. "What are we going to do with him?"

"Well, if he's been a bad boy we'll have to hand him over to the police so everything hinges on why he wrote the card in Anthony's name. I mean, there is the possibility he just did it for fun but I don't think that's the case, is it, John?"

They heard a vehicle park down the side of the house followed by the slamming of doors.

"Excellent. Sounds like Freddie's back."

Within seconds Freddie entered the house along with Max who had driven back with him so that she could pick up her mother's car. Both gasped at the sight of Dilly kneeling on John's chest.

"Just in time," Dilly stood up, "John's going to explain a few things to us." She gripped his hands and pulled him to his feet. "Sit down."

Scowling at the bunch of dried lavender now lying on the rug, John brushed down his clothing. He then sat in one of the three armchairs. "It's not what you think. At least. Oh dear."

Dilly sat down in the chair beside John lest he try to escape. Freddie and Max, both confused, took seats at the table where they turned their chairs to face the clearly shaken historian. To explain the reason behind the situation, Amelia passed them the two cards she held in her hands for them to see the likeness. She then sat down in the remaining armchair.

"Right, John. Would you care to just tell us what this is all about or would you rather we fired questions at you?" Dilly spoke in her sternest schoolmarm voice.

"I'll explain. I think that'd be best," he lowered his head and looked at his hands. "But first let me say that I wouldn't have hurt you, Dilly. I panicked and despite how it seemed, I never would have hurt you. Please believe me because I'm truly sorry."

Dilly nodded, conscious of tears welling in his eyes. "So what's this all about, John?"

"Well when you first mentioned looking into the Brays' history I was happy to go along with it. I thought I was safe, you see. I mean, I knew Anthony was dead and was confident Cyril would never come clean, especially after all these years. Sadly I was wrong. On the other hand, maybe it's for the best. Him confessing, I mean. Anyway, it all started back in 1975 on the day Anthony came here. Not that I knew then because I didn't see him. Well, not 'til later that day. You see, when the hit and run took place I was on my way to the pub, and as I approached the bus stop I saw someone standing there beneath the streetlamp but thought nothing of it. Then suddenly there was a screech of brakes and a scream. I stopped walking and watched as someone got out of a car and ran round to the pavement...."

"...Hang on, hang on," interrupted Dilly, "You told us you were away when the hit and run took place."

John hung his head. "I lied and gambled on the fact you wouldn't find me out."

"Okay. Carry on then."

"Well he, the driver, then jumped back in the car and drove away. Needless to say I recognised the car and the driver. Unfortunately so did the chap at the bus stop. Not sure how as it would only have been a fleeting glance but then the window was down and I suppose the light from the streetlamp was just about enough for him to see. Back then Cyril did stand out in a crowd. Shoulder-length, curly copper-coloured hair, a goatee beard and John Lennon type glasses. A bit different to now."

"Yes, there are a few pictures of him in the Brays' old photo albums," said Dilly.

"Yes, of course."

"So what happened next?" Amelia asked.

"Anthony ran across the road and must have seen Frank lying there, his head on the kerbstone in a pool of blood. In anger he waving his fist and shouted after the car, which by then was quite a way down the road, 'I know who you are, mate,' he said, 'and I'm ringing the police'. He then headed for the phone box by the bus stop. I panicked. I couldn't let him ring the police. Couldn't have Cyril arrested. So I ran after him. At the top of the steps I caught up with him, grabbed him by the arm and in a scuffle I pushed him down the steps so no-one would see us. I wanted to reason with him, you see. Honest, I just wanted to reason with him. But that wasn't possible because the fall knocked him out and then I realised he wasn't breathing." John lifted his head, there was sadness in his eyes. "I should have left him there, then when someone found him they'd have thought he'd fallen down the steps. Which in a way he had. But no, being a fool I picked him up, slung him over my shoulder and carried him across the beach. Fortunately he wasn't heavy. Couldn't have weighed more than nine stone and by then I'd been fishing for twenty years and so was pretty strong. Anyway, I carried him into the cave out of sight and planned to return the next day to bury him. As I walked back across the beach, I heard sirens up on the street. I told myself to act casually. I then climbed up the steps and made my way along the road. When I reached the vehicles with flashing lights I even stopped to ask Maurice what had happened. He told me about Frank and I feigned shock and horror. By then a considerable crowd was gathering, no doubt brought out by the sirens. Needless to say I didn't go to the pub. I wanted to make myself scarce so went home instead. Poured myself a large brandy and reflected on what I'd done. The next morning I was up before it was light and with a torch and spade I went to the beach to bury the poor sod. At the time I didn't even know who he was. I assumed he was someone visiting. Before I buried him I went through his pockets. I found a wallet and driving licence with the name Anthony Hammond on it. It meant nothing to me and then I remembered he'd recognised Cyril. I didn't know how or why and at that time it didn't really matter. I put the wallet in my pocket and then dug a shallow grave above the high water mark and placed him in it and covered him with sand. I then gathered together lots of cobbles and pebbles and scattered them over and around his grave. By the time I'd finished it was getting light and sun was rising over the sea. Had the situation been different I'd have sat and watched it but as it was I scuttled off home. Didn't want to be seen with the spade, you see. When I got home I remembered the driving licence and thought if he could drive he'd probably have a car in the village somewhere and after a while someone would report it as being abandoned. But then I remembered he'd been waiting for a bus so assumed he'd come down by bus, train or whatever. A few days later I saw Bert and told him I was sorry to hear about his dad. He thanked me and then told me of the day's events. How Anthony had turned up and upset his dad and he'd gone off to the pub in a huff. During that conversation everything fell into place and I knew who Anthony Hammond was, but of course I couldn't say. The next day Ethel died and I vowed I'd take my secret to the grave."

"But why, John. Why did you go to such lengths to protect Cyril?" Dilly's voice had softened.

He looked up. "It wasn't to protect Cyril, it was to protect Carol."

"Carol. I don't understand."

"Carol was a local girl. She grew up in the village and were a year younger than me. She was pretty, witty, outgoing and really popular. A leader to us kids and we all adored her. I was the opposite; shy, pasty-faced, weak and bespectacled. I lacked confidence and got tongue-tied. Some of the other kids ignored me, teased me. Wanted to leave me out of things. Called me names. But not Carol. She always stood up for me and insisted I was included. It was her kindness that changed the attitude of others and eventually I was accepted as one of them. When we grew up we remained friends. I used to fantasise that one day I'd wake up handsome and she'd fall madly in love with me. But of course it never happened and then she met Cyril. We all went to the wedding and I'd never seen her look so happy. And seeing her happy made me happy, despite the heartache I felt. A few months later she discovered she was pregnant. She was overjoyed. They were both overjoyed and then she had a miscarriage. I've never seen anyone go from looking a picture of health to sickly in such a short space of time. She lost her appetite. Lost weight and almost lost the will to live, but eventually she pulled herself together and started to laugh again. When she discovered she was pregnant a second time we were all happy for her and Cyril of course and we treated her with kid gloves and that's why on that night in 1975 when Cyril knocked down Frank, I couldn't let Cyril face arrest."

"Because you didn't want her to lose the baby."

"That's right. Baby Emma."

Dilly took John's hand. "I'm so sorry. Sorry that Anthony died before you had a chance to reason with him and sorry that you've had to live with this guilt all these years."

"Me too," said Amelia.

"But you didn't kill him," said Max, "you pushed him and he fell. It was *never* your intention to kill him."

John nodded. "I know, and as I said I should have left him at the foot of the steps for someone else to find or even pretended I'd found him myself. Not that that would have been very convincing with it being dark. But I didn't do either. Like a fool I buried him so I'm guilty of not reporting an accident and unlawful burial."

Max sighed. "Yes, I suppose so."

"Out of curiosity, what did you do with the wallet?" Amelia asked.

"I went to Plymouth and took it to the address on the driving licence. They were paper ones back then. Licences, that is. I pretended I'd found it on the pavement outside Marks and Spencer. I wanted to make sure no-one came looking for him in Cornwall, you see. As it was his flatmates had no idea where he was or where he'd been. They'd not seen him for several days of course and assumed he'd scarpered to get away from some female or other who was trying to get her clutches into him. They kept the wallet anyway and said they'd give it to him if and when he got back. I didn't tell them who I was or where I lived and so I never heard anything more."

"And the Christmas card," said Dilly, "Why did you send that?"

"To clear Anthony's name. I thought it was the least I could do. I mean, the poor lad was innocent and I reasoned that if you believed he was planning to come back here in 1976 then you'd think he obviously had a clear conscience and so had nothing to do with the hit and run. Of course, that was before he was found and had it not been for the bracelet and Ivy helping with DNA, he'd never have been identified."

"And if it wasn't for the storm, the sea would never have exposed his remains," said Freddie. "In a way that was rotten luck."

"It was because I know the sea well and never in my wildest dreams could I have imagined it going that far up the beach. Those caves are usually bone dry," he smiled weakly, "No pun intended."

Amelia shuddered. "It's eerie too that the storm was called Albert."

"Very," agreed Dilly. She turned to John, "and Popeye, did you come up with that name?"

The colour drained from John's face. "Well yes and no. I did but I didn't intend to. Something sort of pushed me, guided my fingers like. I must admit I thought it was funny when it happened, but then I was devastated when I learned that Cyril grew spinach and Frank referred to him as Popeye. It still makes me shudder just thinking about it. That's why on the second boozy night, having already spelled out Olive Oyl, I tried to spell out Bluto; to make light of the Popeye reference, you understand. But Ernie guessed and it threw me out. I had no choice then but to go for Bert."

Dilly sighed. "Oh, what a mess."

"It is and what do we do now?" Freddie asked, "Forget what John's just told us and carry on as normal or tell the police?"

"No, we can't tell the police," Max was horrified at the thought, "Poor John would spend the rest of his life in prison."

John shook his head. "Thanks, Max, that means a lot but none of you need to do anything because now it's all come out I intend to hand myself in. I should have done it years ago."

"Well, there's no rush," urged Dilly, "I suggest you keep quiet and think about it for a few days."

"I will. I'll give it until the end of the week and then pop along and see Maurice. I know he's retired but he's a good bloke and I'd like him to know just what happened before I go to the police station."

Chapter Twenty-Four

The following day, John set out to take Ben for his usual morning walk and because there was no wind and the weather was fine, he decided the conditions were ideal for a stroll across the beach. The agony of confessing to his crime had deprived him of sleep. He was tired, his eyes ached, his head ached and he hoped the rhythm of the sea might help soothe his troubled brow.

Meanwhile, Ernie was already on the beach with Oscar and was walking back from the slipway when he spotted John on the pavement above, his hand on the wall by the flight of steps near to the bus stop. Wanting to speak to him and say how sorry he was to hear what had happened way back in 1975, he watched as the elderly man put his foot on the first step. Simultaneously, a gull landed on top of the wall and Ben, eager to see it off, leapt up towards it. The gull angrily squawked, flapped its wings and flew away towards the sea. In the commotion, Ben's lead tangled around his master's ankles and without realising, John stepped forwards, stumbled and fell head first down the steep steps onto the cobbles below.

Concerned for the historian's wellbeing, Ernie dashed across the beach, phone in hand ready to call for help. Not far behind Ernie, was Peter Goodman, the vicar who had also witnessed the accident. They arrived at John's motionless body together: his grey hair red with blood seeping from a deep head wound. Ernie knelt down by John's side and clasped his friend's frail hand. "Hold on there, John, hold on." With his free hand he punched 999 into his phone and asked for an ambulance and then trying to keep the anguish from his voice, gently stroked John's cheek, "Stay awake, John, stay awake. Help's on its way."

The vicar, eager that the ambulance stop at the correct place went up onto the road to flag it down.

"It's too late, Ernie. It's too late," John slowly moved his head and focused his eyes on Ernie's face, "My time's up and rightly so, but I want you to promise me that you'll go and see Maurice and tell him what I did. I was going to go this afternoon, but now, well, it's too late."

Ernie looked up to make sure the vicar was out of earshot. "We don't need to tell Maurice or anyone else what happened," he whispered, "Surely it would be best to let sleeping dogs lie?"

"No, no, I need to meet my maker with a clear conscience. Promise me, Ernie."

"Okay. I promise."

"Thank you," John smiled, and squeezed Ernie's hand, "And please take care of Ben. He's a good boy and a loyal friend." He released Ernie's hand and weakly stroked the Labrador lying by his side. He then returned his gaze to Ernie. "You know it's true what they say. It must be because silly old me fell down the same steps as I pushed Anthony down. Yes, it's true alright. What goes around comes around."

Ernie stayed with John, holding his hand until the ambulance arrived and the vicar guided its crew to the steps. The paramedics tried to revive him but eventually gave up and pronounced him dead. As the vicar with a heavy heart said a prayer for his friend, a police car arrived. After the ambulance had driven away with John, Ernie and the vicar, choked with emotion, told the police who John was and where he lived. That he had a brother, Bruce, who was his next of kin, and how the accident had happened. Ernie then returned home with Oscar and

John's Labrador, Ben in tow. After telling Amelia what had happened, the two of them walked round to Lavender Cottage to break the news to Dilly. They took Ben with them just in case Oscar objected to another dog in his domain.

On hearing of his dying wish, Dilly offered to go with Amelia and Ernie to see Maurice so that together they missed no relevant details.

The following day, Ernie went to visit John's brother, Bruce at Elm House for two reasons. One to see how he was faring having received news of his brother's death from the police and two, to ask if he wanted to give Ben a home. Bruce said that as much as he loved the Labrador, he wasn't fit enough to give him the exercise he'd need and asked Ernie if he could find him a good home. On hearing this, Dilly stepped in. Many years before she had owned a black Labrador and said she would be delighted to look after Ben for the rest of his days.

The case of the body in the cave went through the usual police channels and was then closed. The only details released to the press were that the person responsible for Anthony Hammond's demise could not be charged as he was deceased. No name was publicised and with no living person to pursue the media lost interest. Anthony Hammond was then laid to rest alongside his cousin Bert, and Dilly moved by the whole episode, instructed Reg Rogers to make a memorial stone for him at her expense.

The service at the crematorium for John Martin drew a large crowd from Trenwalloe Sands for he was a much liked member of the community. When John's ashes were returned to his brother, Bruce, Bruce asked Ziggy Lugg to help arrange John's final resting place. A few days later, Ziggy took out a small party in Sassy Sal and scattered his ashes at sea.

Cyril Thomas was charged with failing to report an accident but not with dangerous driving as Frank Bray had been in the road at the time and witnesses at the pub said he was drinking heavily and in a foul mood. Cyril received a suspended sentence and was free to live out his final years with only his conscience to punish him.

Chapter Twenty-Five

On Saint Valentine's Day, as Ben lay on the rug in front of the Truburn at Lavender Cottage, the back door opened. "Coo-ee. Only me." Recognising the voice, Ben raised his head and wagged his tail.

"Come in, Amelia." Dilly was in the living room checking to see if any seeds in trays on the window sill had germinated. "Look at this, the little lobelia are coming up. I find it so exciting when this happens and convince myself that spring is just around the corner."

"You sound like Ernie," Amelia leaned forwards and stroked Ben's head, "His parsley's coming up and so are his peppers."

"Wonderful. I've sowed white lavender seeds too to grow amongst the mauve, should they succeed, but they've yet to germinate," Dilly placed the lobelia seedlings back inside the polythene bag. "Coffee?"

"Yes, please, that would be lovely, but the reason I've called is to say I popped in the charity shop first thing this morning with some books and while I was there asked if they'd like Bert and his family's old clothes. I said some were nearly vintage. They seemed quite keen and said to drop it all in and they'd go through it."

"Bless you. That's wonderful and as you know it's something I've been meaning to do for a while, but with all the distractions it got pushed to one side."

"That's what I thought. Anyway, if you want I'll help you pack it up and we can take it down there on Monday. Best to strike while the iron's hot."

"We'll do that then as soon as we've had coffee."

Because there was no heating in the small bedroom, where the clothing lay in heaps on the floor, Dilly and Amelia made several trips with arms full and transported it all down into the living room where they dropped it on the rug by the fire beside Ben who eyed it with suspicion. Dilly then took a roll of black bin liners from a drawer in the sideboard to bag things up.

"Where do we start?" Amelia picked up a flat cap which she recognised as one Bert used to wear.

Dilly scratched her head. "How about we sort it into two piles? One of chap's stuff and the other ladies."

"Yes, that sounds logical so we'll do that."

"Good, and if you see anything that takes your fancy, Amelia, please help yourself."

"I might just do that. I seldom buy new clothes because we don't really go anywhere but it's always nice to ring the changes."

"My thoughts entirely, but lots of these ladies' things look too big for me so I assume Ethel was well-built. Probably muscular too with all the spinach she ate."

Amelia chuckled. "Well if she was big, they're bound to fit me."

Dilly held up a floral dress, a combination of red roses and lavender. "How about this? It's really pretty." She passed the dress to Amelia.

"Oh, my goodness. If it fits this would be ideal to wear tonight but it's too late now to get it washed, dried and ironed."

Dilly looked at the clock. "Yes I suppose it is, but where are you off to tonight?"

"Just the pub. Gail and Robert always put on a special menu for Valentine's Day and so we've booked a table for that. Ernie's a real romantic. He's taken me out every year since we've been together."

"Lovely, and if that's the case you can save the dress for next year."

The men's clothing was less interesting than the ladies. They separated the garments into shirts, jackets, trousers, suits, ties and coats. Vests and pants they put to one side to be used as rags along with work clothes that had seen better days.

"Before we pack them in the bags we ought to go through the pockets," said Amelia, "there are bound to be a few grubby handkerchiefs in the men's pockets."

"And probably old fag packets too." Dilly held up a jacket, "This is a nice suit. Nice fabric. Do you think it might have been Bert's?"

"No, it looks too small. Bert was quite dumpy. Having said that he could have been more slender when young and still working."

When Dilly put her fingers inside the breast pocket she touched a piece of card and pulled it out. It was an old black and white photograph of a young woman. "Aha, who might this be?"

"Joan? Ethel when young? Might even be Elizabeth Bray who loved lavender and named this place."

"No, if you remember, Elizabeth died in in 1940 and the date on this is 1958. Same with Ethel. She was born in 1913 so in '58 she'd have been forty-five. I'd say this young lady is not much older than twenty. As for it being Joan, judging by the picture we found in the motorbike's manual, I can't see any resemblance."

"And she was born in 1918 anyway, so the dates wouldn't fit there either."

"Of course, yes. I guess we'll never know then. But I'll put it to one side anyway. If we take it to the pub and show it around someone might recognise her."

Amelia sighed. "I bet John would have recognised her and if not he'd have endeavoured to find out."

"Yes, yes, he would." Dilly cast a loving glance at Ben whose head was tilted to one side as though he understood who they were talking about.

Before she folded the jacket, Dilly checked the pocket for anything else; tucked in the bottom corner she felt a small metal object and pulled out a ring. "Oh my goodness. Look at this, Amelia. Do you think these are real diamonds?" She placed it on the palm of her hand so both could see it better.

"Most likely, yes. I mean the gold looks to be a good quality."

Dilly gasped. "It does and I've just realised who the young lady in the picture must be. If I'm not mistaken she'll be Max's great aunt. The one who many years ago was engaged to Bert."

The ladies were filling up the last bag of the clothing when Freddie returned home having been out to weigh up a plastering job. When shown the ring and photograph, he was intrigued. "So what do you intend to do with them?"

"I'd don't know. What do you suggest?"

"I think if it were me I'd give them to Max. After all Mary Lucy Trelawney nee Pascoe was her great aunt, and as Mary told Max all about the broken engagement it seems the right thing to do."

"That's a nice idea and I'm impressed you remember the aunt's name."

"So am I, especially as I reeled it off without thinking about it."

"Will you drop them in some time?" Dilly hoped he'd say yes.

"Of course, no problem. In fact I'll go after lunch. Helen said to call in for a cuppa when I'm out that way so I'm sure I'd be welcome."

Freddie left for Hilltop Farm just after two. He parked in the yard near the duck pond and was about to knock on the farmhouse door when he heard Max's voice drifting across from the fields. He followed the sound of laughter and found her chatting over the fence to the donkey.

"Yay, look Nicholas, we have a visitor," she pecked Freddie on the cheek as he drew up by her side.

Freddie held up his empty hands. "Sorry, Nick, but I don't have any carrots for you."

"Don't worry, he's had more than enough for now, haven't you, Mr Piggy Wiggy?"

Nicholas nuzzled Freddie's neck. "I don't think he agrees."

"No I'm sure he doesn't, but what brings you here on this fine sunny afternoon?"

"I have a surprise for you," Freddie reached into his pocket, pulled out the ring and placed it on the palm of his hand, "This."

Max's cheeks flushed. "Are you asking me to marry you?"

"What?" he laughed, "Oh, good heavens, no. Why on earth would you think that?"

A look of disappointment crossed her face. "Because it's St. Valentine's Day, I suppose."

"Oh, oh, I see," Freddie realised he was in a very awkward position, "Well, I suppose if you'd like me to, I could ask you to marry me."

Max frowned. "Let's start again and this time explain the situation better because I don't understand where you're coming from. I mean, why the ring? It doesn't make sense."

"Ah, yes, I can see it from your point of view now," Freddie looked down at the palm of his hand. "Well you see, it's like this. I found it. Actually that's not true because Dilly and Amelia found it and we all agreed that I should give it to you. Not in a, *asking you to marry me* way though. More in a, *it used to belong to you* way. Well not to you, but a member of your family. Your aunt actually. Mary Lucy Trelawney nee Pascoe."

The penny dropped. "Oh, I see. So you think this is the engagement ring that Great Aunt Mary gave back to Bert." She took it from his hand and held it up in the sunlight, "How sad that he kept it. Beautiful too though."

"It was in the breast pocket of a suit and along with the ring was this," Freddie pulled out the photograph and gave it to Max, "We assume this lady is Mary."

"Well, I never. Come on. Let's go and show Mum. She knew Mary and the two got on very well."

"Put the ring on your finger," chuckled Freddie, "and then you can pretend we're engaged."

Max scowled. "Don't be silly, Freddie. She'd be devastated when she learned it was a joke."

"Really?"

"Yes, of course. She's longing to see me married and she rather likes you."

When Freddie arrived back at Lavender Cottage he found Dilly asleep in an armchair by the fire and Ben curled up by her feet. As he closed the door, Dilly's eyes flashed open. "Goodness me. Was I asleep?"

"Yes, I tried not to wake you."

"Well, I'm glad you did. Taking an afternoon nap is what old people do."

He kissed the top of her head and then sat down in the chair opposite. "You'll never be old even though you'll be seventy-three next birthday."

"Hmm, don't remind me," Dilly sat up straight, "Anyway, I was probably sleepy because while you were out Ivy called round," Dilly chuckled, "Would you believe with her she brought a pack of lavender tealeaves? The reason being she wanted to know if I'd be her guinea pig and let her read the residue in my cup."

"Lavender tealeaves. Yuck! That sounds ghastly."

"Yes, it was a bit odd, I must admit. Apparently she bought the leaves on-line awhile back having read that lavender tea increases psychic awareness and clairvoyant energy."

"I remember John saying something along those lines," chuckled Freddie.

"Yes, yes, he did. Anyway, she tried it out on herself, but, bless her, said she didn't think its magic worked if the person reading the leaves was the same person who drank the tea, and whose fortune she was telling. If you see what I mean."

"Well I can't see that it'd make any difference as I'm sure it's all nonsense." Freddie cast a glance at the picture of Bert's grandmother, "Sorry Elizabeth. No offence meant."

Dilly chuckled. "I don't think she'd mind. You know, the one thing I really regret is we never got to meet Bert although I feel he's here, watching us, just like the rest of the family and I hope he and they approve of what we've done and will do in the near future."

"I'm sure they do and will." Freddie nodded towards the arm of Dilly's chair. "But why have you fished Bert's old toy ambulance out?"

"Ah, that's to remind me to tell you what Ivy said. Although you mustn't repeat it because she was told it in confidence by the vicar."

"Sounds intriguing."

"Well, it is a bit because it answers something I've wondered about now and again. Do you remember when I first told you about this house and how Bert's will stated everything be left to the village church even though he wasn't a churchgoer."

"Yes, I remember."

"Well many years ago when Bert was a lad of ten, the village school children held their annual carol service in the church as usual. At the end of the service as people left they dropped money onto a collection plate by the font. Amongst the change was a ten shilling note and Bert after checking no-one was looking, grabbed the note and stuffed it in his pocket intending to use it to buy a new fishing rod. However, as soon as he got outside he felt guilty and so crept back inside and when near the plate bent down and pretended he'd found it on the floor. Nearby, was the vicar's wife, who touched by his action gave him half a crown from her own purse and told him that honesty is always the best policy. Because the coin was dated 1935 and so the year of his birth, he thought it very special. However, he always felt she knew the truth and for that reason her words kept him on the straight and narrow throughout his life. We know this because when the vicar and his family were preparing to leave the parish in 1957, Bert went to see the vicar's wife to confess his guilt and as he left the Vicarage, he told her that one day he'd put his wrong to right."

"I wonder if that's the same vicar's wife who played Prince Charming in the church's production of Cinderella."

"Sybil Keating. The lady with the lovely legs. Yes, it was her and if you remember it was said at John's history night in the pub that she was our current vicar's grandmother, so that's how he knew about the carol service money. But of course he would never tell his parishioners, despite their curiosity, and so they remain baffled to this day."

"But he told Ivy."

"Yes, and she told me but it must go no further than these four walls."

Freddie sighed. "Poor old John. I think he and his history evenings will be missed greatly and deep down I'm sure he was a caring man."

"I agree and I know for one that I'll miss him, and you miss him too, don't you, Ben?"

Ben stood up and rested his head on Dilly's lap.

"I'm sure he does and it's a blessing he's taken to you so well."

"Yes. It'd be heart wrenching if the poor chap pined for John."

"Hmm, so out of curiosity, what's half a crown in today's money?"

Dilly laughed. "It was two shillings and sixpence back then which would be twelve and a half pence today. So in the mid nineteen forties that would have been a nice bit of money. In fact if Bert was ten then that'd be 1945 and so the first Christmas after the ending of the Second World War."

"Wow! A long time ago then." Feeling warm, Freddie removed his jacket, "But that doesn't explain the toy ambulance."

"It does because the half-crown's in here." She handed the toy vehicle to Freddie who tipped the coin into the palm of his hand and removed the small piece of old Christmas paper. "Wow, very impressive. Quite heavy too. A complete contrast to the coins we have today."

"Yes, the old money was much nicer but today's decimal system is far simpler to understand."

Freddie returned the coin to the back of the ambulance. "So what did the tealeaves say? I'm assuming Ivy read them for you."

"What! Oh, you know the usual fortune telling nonsense," Dilly chuckled, "Ivy said she could see wedding bells which actually made us both laugh. She even suggested Orville King might be a possible suitor."

"Wedding bells," the colour had gone from Freddie's face.

"Yes, so silly. As if Orville or anyone else for that matter would want to marry an old dear like me. Which reminds me: what did Max say when she saw the engagement ring?"

"What…umm…, well, all sorts of things and she was touched that Bert had kept it all these years. We showed Helen the photo and she confirmed it was Mary."

"So what do you think she'll do with it? The ring, that is."

Freddie tried not to smirk. "She, she's going to wear it. In fact she's wearing it now."

"That's nice."

"Yes, to our surprise it was a perfect fit and might have been made for her."

"Which finger is she wearing it on?" Dilly was suddenly aware of a twinkle in Freddie's eyes.

"Third finger, left hand."

"But…"

He chuckled, recalling his visit to the farm. "I asked her in a very roundabout way to marry me and she said yes."

Dilly sprang from her chair and gave him a hug. "Oh, Freddie, I'm so happy for you. She's a lovely, lovely girl."

"She is, but don't you think it's weird? I mean, how did Ivy know? It only happened an hour or so ago. I'm referring of course to her mention of wedding bells."

"Goodness only knows," Dilly left her chair and picked up the bone china cup from the top of the cooker where she'd left it. "Here's the tealeaves. What do you see?"

Freddie took the cup. "Err, tealeaves." He sniffed the contents, "That is to say, lavender tealeaves."

"Same for me," Dilly sat back down, "I think Ivy was just trying her hand at matchmaking."

"Most likely." A concerned look crossed Freddie's face, "I'm worried about you. I mean, will you be alright on your own with me gone?"

"I shall miss you of course, but I've lived alone for many years, and remember that was my original plan when I moved down here. Anyway, I have Ben now, so I'll not be alone."

"True, and Amelia and Ernie are next door." Freddie stood and took mugs from the kitchen cabinet. "Time for tea, I think. Common-or-garden teabag tea."

Dilly leaned back her head. "So this little adventure has all turned out well. We now know who knocked down Frank and who took poor Anthony's life. Julien's coming round tomorrow to measure up and draw up plans for the new extension and you're going to marry lovely Max."

"We've both made friends too and I love singing with the choir."

"Yes, and soon Bert's dahlias will be coming up. I shall take great care of them when they do and put some of the flowers on his grave, and Anthony's too."

"And through lavender the spirit of the Brays lives on."

Dilly chuckled. "I hope so and I've just remembered, Ivy said the vicar was in a very good mood when she saw him yesterday because outline planning for Albert's Hall has been approved, so the name of Bray will live on even though there are none of them left."

"Really. That makes me feel quite emotional."

"That's what I thought, but as far as Ivy's wedding bells prediction goes we must see that as pure coincidence. I mean, she can no more predict the future through tealeaves than I can fly."

As Freddie handed Dilly a mug of tea, there was a knock on the door. Freddie answered and after a few minutes returned to the room carrying a bunch of red roses. "That was a delivery man and these are for you."

Dilly took the flowers and looked at the attached card. A huge smile lit up her face. The card read:

Lavender's mauve, Dilly, Dilly,
Its leaves are green,
I am a King, Dilly, Dilly,
Please be my queen.

THE END